SHORT STORIES AND POEMS VOLUME 1

A COLLECTION OF SHORT STORIES AND POEMS

GRAHAME ANDERSON

BLUE TAO

ISBN 978-1-912872-07-7

Created with Vellum

INTRODUCTION

This collection has come together somewhat randomly, similar to all the poems and stories I write. My creative juices come and go and I tend to work with them when it happens rather than force a story or poem out. It's not unusual for me to go three or four months with nothing written and then, without knowing why, I can write twenty items every week for a month.

That's what I love about life, the whole wonderful, crazy, unexpectedness of it.

This collection is a real mixed bag covering, love, death, fantasy, spiritualism, childhood, pets and of course Mother Nature and the moon - my two favourite subjects.

Please have a browse through these pages - if you don't like a particular story skip to the next and save time, I'm not expecting readers to like them all.

One thing I'm always trying to do is to encourage people to be creative and have a go at writing. It comes with the territory of being a member of Greenock Writers' Club and Scottish Association of Writers. Writing is one of these wonderful arts where with nothing more than a pencil and piece of paper you can create worlds that come alive for others and give them every emotional struggle you choose to.

Why not throw caution to the wind and see what you can create, it's fun. And whatever you create, don't judge it too harshly. Remember, you have created something that never existed before and there are plenty of people out there who are sure to love it. So get writing. An example we do in writing class is to write for five minutes from three random words/phrases.

Here are your phrases: The Moon, A Mysterious Woman and an Antique Shop. Just write for five or ten minutes and see what you have created. You can repeat this every week for a month, whatever suits.

One last thing if you want me to read your story I'd be happy to do so as long as it's not over 500 words. That's my caveat in the event someone sends me a 100,000 word novel. Email me from my website www.grahameanderson.co.uk

Peace and Love

Grahame

ABOUT THE AUTHOR

Grahame Anderson is the author of *The Lighthouse Keepers,* and *The Best Seat in the Universe*. He is currently working on a number of other writing projects.

You can visit him at
www.grahameanderson.co.uk

Email: info@grahameanderson.com

Grahame lives with his wife, Brenda and two sons in the small town of Gourock on the west coast of Scotland. He has been involved in print and media for over forty years. When not writing Grahame will be listening to music or reading books.

CONTENTS

1

POM POMS

The streets are full of pom-poms
Woolly hats are coming on
The cold is biting through us
I'm sure our summer's gone

They remind me of my childhood
reading Pooh, tiddly pom - tiddly pom
But I certainly don't feel like bouncing
As winter brings its' storms

My mind drifts back to my childhood
Primary five, long-legged, Miss Ward
She gave us all a cardboard ring
With some wool, we got to work

We wound our wool around that ring
We used scissors to snip the wool and things
Thirty pom-poms made, some fluffy, some thin
But the memories that day is of our cheesy grins

The streets are full of pom-poms
And I can't help myself, but say
That a memory of fifty years ago
Can still make my winter's day

2

WHISPERS ON A BREEZE

Can you hear them, those whispers, or is it only me?
I'm sure, they've been trying to reach me, sending words
upon the breeze
Is it possible, I'm dreaming, or confusing the rustling of
the leaves
My heart, is oh so sure, my parents want to contact me

Hear that voice, it sounds so clear? That was definitely
my mum

With dad in the background, sounds like they're still
having fun
It's been so long, since I saw them, and I have so much
to say
About our kids, and how our lives changed the moment
they went away

We're here son, can't you see us? We're over here behind
the veil
We've been watching, all along, from this beautiful hidden
trail
Reach forward, touch our fingers, its the best we can do
To hold you, once more, and confirm the love we have
for you

Can you hear them, those whispers, or is it only me?
They're trying hard to reach us, leaving messages, not
everyone can see
Believe me, they're real, and not the rustling of some
leaves
Behind the veil, between our worlds, they keep a watch on
you and me

3
WINTER IS COMING

Clear blue skies, welcome calm waters
A boat cuts through, a flock of gulls can't help but follow
Frost grows thicker, resting on all that lies still
A cold winter morn, and yet, no snow on the hills

4

EMPTY BEDS

Tracer fire screaming, across darkened skies
Young soldiers terrified, not wanting to die
They face an enemy in front or their captain behind
An unfair choice, life or death on the front line

Sweethearts photos held close to their chests
A promise and a whisper, in love they're so blessed
To be home wrapped in arms, feeling warm in their nest
Instead of freezing in a ditch filled with blood and last
breaths

Shell blasts deafen, men stagger to open ground
Bullets rip through them as more artillery pounds
This land they defend with the price of their lives
For us to have freedom from their sacrifice

They never had careers or homes of their own
Denied a life full of love and children to watch grow
Their parents left grieving, most questioning WHY?
They've only rooms with empty beds, where they lay
down to cry

5
BIG TAMS SPIRITUAL ADVENTURE (PART ONE)

BIG TAM STRUGGLED AS HE WALKED ALONG THE DIRT TRACK, HIS hiking boots felt too heavy for his skinny legs. He tried to remember how long he'd been on this journey. It must have been at least six months.

It was hot, far hotter than anything he'd experienced before. His mouth was bone dry, and he tried hard to create enough saliva to wet his lips. His breathing felt laboured and he struggled with each intake of breath. As a Scotsman, he preferred the cold weather to this uncomfortable heat.

He wiped away the sweat trickling down his brow and leaned against a rickety wooden fence. His legs were giving way and beginning to shake. Tam steadied himself and sat down on the grass, it was brownish yellow and coarse to the touch.

He felt exhausted, the smallest tasks in this heat seemed to sap all his energy.

He unlaced his boots and felt a sense of relief. He tried to kick them off as his arms had become too weak. He struggled for a while until with one last heave he pushed them off. He pushed his hand inside one of his boots fumbling around. He searched for what had been the source of so much pain. He pinched his fingers around a tiny stone.

'Jeez, there you are. Look at the size of you, you little shit. You felt like a boulder under my foot.'

Taking aim he tossed the stone in the direction of a small beetle coursing its way back home along the uneven road.

Tam peeled his socks off to inspect his feet. The cotton had stuck tight to his skin because of the mixture of dried blood and sweat. It felt like pulling off sticky tape as he released his socks from his skin. He sniffed the dirty socks and withdrew again, the smell was overpowering.

'Jeezus!'

He placed his socks on the fence to air while he nursed his battered feet. He'd never had trouble with them before and now they looked like they'd been to war. Two blisters were swollen ready to burst while the other three were weeping a clear liquid and blood. With his pocket-knife, he stabbed the large blisters. Liquid oozed out running down his heel. He dabbed his feet on the grass. As the blisters deflated, they left a rippled lump of white skin.

'Thank God.' he said out loud, his breathing less intense.

His fingers probed between each toe, massaging and finding debris that didn't smell right. From his backpack, he fetched a hankie. With the cool cotton material, he polished back and forth in a sawing motion, drying between each toe. He felt pleased giving them the attention they needed. With his feet stimulated he was already feeling better. He pressed his thumbs hard into his arches making him scream inside as he massaged the tension from his aching feet. His toenails were too long making his boots uncomfortable. He needed nail clippers or his boots wouldn't fit.

Thinking back on this journey he tried to make sense of how he arrived here. It seemed different from what he'd planned but he couldn't quite put his finger on it.

He watched the farm labourers work the land. A white ox whose rib cage was visible dragged a heavy plough behind it. A man steered the animal with the use of a large cane. At the far end of the field, women were hand cutting the long grass with scythes and binding it together with twine. They stacked their bundles in large neat piles near the edge of the field. Tam wondered how they managed to work in this heat.

A pungent smell drifted towards him on the breeze. His nostrils were filled with a heavy fragrance. He looked up to see a tree in full bloom. The flowers in a multitude of colours opened wide capturing the sun's rays. The perfume was intoxicating, what his dad would have called a 'nancy' smell. He stepped over the fence to get a closer look, his kilt catching on a stray nail.

'For god's sake, my good kilt.'

He inspected the tear to his 'worse for wear' clan tartan kilt. It was fixable, once he reached a town. He'd learnt one thing in India, the local people knew how to mend clothes. He reached up to the tree and picked some large flowers and gathered some petals on the ground into his kilt.

He was more careful scaling the fence the second time careful not to drop his flowers. He placed petals in his socks in the hope they would reduce the foul smell. He sniffed under his arms and like his socks it wasn't pretty. He couldn't remember when he'd last washed, but it was at least ten days ago. The starvation angered him most. He had gone past the hunger stage after four days of nothing and was beginning to feel the effects. If he didn't eat today he was sure to collapse.

Two men walked past dressed in bright flowing robes, they put their palms together and bowed. 'Namaste' they said in unison.

'Same to you guys - whatever.'

He rubbed the petals under his arms, across his chest and on his face, he smelled good. The odour attracted the attention of a number of large black bees. He swung his arms at them, grabbed his socks and boots and ran down the road as fast as he could. Once he'd gone fifty yards he was sure it was safe to put his socks and boots back on.

His head was so hot he thought he would faint. He started to drift off seeing things that he knew weren't there. From nowhere a gust of freezing cold wind came over him. It felt cool and exactly what he needed. He couldn't fathom how a cold breeze could cut through the heat.

Up ahead in a field he spied a large sprawling tree, thick with green leaves. He knew that's where he'd rest under the shade. He crossed the field towards the tree. A large overweight man sat under the shade with his back to the tree trunk. He was sleeping.

Tam felt the coolness from the leaves. He muttered under his breath, 'bloody Indian summer, lasts for eleven months of the year.'

The large man opened an eye at the disturbance.

'Alright bud. I'm Tam, from Scotland.' He stretched out his hand. The man didn't move. He remained silent, his eyes closed, smiling.

Tam shrugged his shoulders and moved around to the other side of the tree. He rested against it trying to regulate his breathing after his sprint, his eyes were closing. The sun seemed to be shining from two directions. Tam could see colour spots floating in front of his eyes like you get when you stare at a very bright object. The light shone in his eyes.

He felt he was slipping in and out of consciousness.

He ventured around the tree again, surprised to see three men, ten feet away, facing the fat man.

'Alright guys, what's happening?' he shouted.

They said nothing.

'Don't be rude guys, that's no way to treat a visitor to your country.'

They ignored him.

'Even in Glasgow my enemies would at least grunt or give me a hard stare. What's wrong with you lot?'

'Silence.' The fat man had spoken.

'Oh, so you can talk. I'm Tam, big Tam to my mates, in case you didn't hear me when you were having forty winks.'

The man withdrew preferring silence. He sat with that smile again.

Tam looked at the fat man and tapped him on the head.

'Hello, I know you're in there, talk to me. What's with the big smile, have you been on the happy juice?'

A monk came forward and took Tam's arm. He put his fingers to his lips. Tam ignored him.

'Listen, big man, I don't want to disturb your afternoon nap but I'm in desperate need of a drink or something. Have you got anything with you? Did your missus give you a packed lunch today you wouldn't mind sharing? '

Another of the monks stepped forward and bowed before Tam.

'It's okay son, you don't need to bow down to me, it's only a kilt. I'm not royalty.'

'We are the disciples and carer of the Buddha. Please don't disturb him.'

'That's funny, you say Buddha, and I say, buddy, same translation by the sounds of it. Why are you lot sitting here watching a man with his eyes closed saying nothing? It's kinda weird don't you think? Haven't you got work to go to?'

'We're here to find answers?'

'Okay, ask me a question? See if I know.'

'You don't understand. Answers through meditation.'

'Definitely, do not go there son. You'll find no answers with that shit. I was on methadone for over three years. Wrecked my brain. Cold turkey is the only answer.'

The monk withdrew.

A crowd made their way along the road. Forty to fifty followers dressed in the same robes moved across the field towards them. Tam decided to sit next to his new buddy and watch the show.

'You better wake up big man, it's getting out of hand. What have you been telling these people? You need to send them packing.'

Tam's stomach rumbled a long low growl.

'Has anybody got anything to drink, or some food, anything? I'm not fussy. I'm on my last legs here.'

The Buddha opened his eyes.

'Welcome to our camp my friend. You are a traveller I see. You can sit over there with our students who seek the path to enlightenment.'

'I've bad news for you guys. This place is full of paths, they're everywhere. And most of them don't have any signs. I'm sure the locals have been using them for firewood. I've travelled thousands of paths since I got here and they all look the same.'

A young monk came forward, but Tam got there first.

'If you don't have any food with you son then I don't want to talk to you. Can you go talk to your friends and find something before I faint. I need something, now.'

The Buddha raised his palm. 'Bring my guest food and water.'

'That's more like it buddy. If you're going to be in charge, act like it.'

A young woman poured a cup of cold water from a flask, came forward and handed it to Tam. He picked it up and let some swirl in his mouth, it brought his mouth to life. He drank some more and it felt like bliss.

'Thanks, hen. Don't mean to be impolite but is there any food where that water came from. I could fair go a succulent piece of chicken.'

The girl ignored his comments and presented him with a tinny, laying it at his feet before backing off.

Tam opened the metal dish and smiled. His favourite, rice pudding. He stuck his nose in to smell it and went off in a dream.

He scooped the pudding into his mouth and savoured every spoonful. His tastebuds were on fire.

'Are you no having any big man? Not that I was sharing. This is too good.'

'No, I'll eat later.'

A fly landed on the dish, Tam swatted it.

'Leave the insect, it does you no harm.'

'They're a pain in the neck. I hate those things. This would be a good country to live if you didn't have these bloody flies. You can't eat anything here without a plague around you.

You lose half of your food before it even gets to your mouth.'

He swatted and flattened the insect on his arm. Buddha held his head and shook it.

'Young man, you've broken the laws of the universe. Please refrain from hurting any living creature and not in my presence. Please sit amongst my disciples and learn my teachings with them?

'No can do big man. I'm staying under the shade. See this ginger hair and freckles, if you haven't noticed my skin looks as if it's bleached white. This body of mine and sunlight don't go well together.

'But this is my tree and where I speak from. I would prefer not to have your interruption.'

'You're getting possessive about the tree big man. I don't see your name on it. I'm staying in the shade.'

The followers were uncomfortable with this visitor. A murmuring grew with some mentioning he had killed.

'So why are these people following you?' Tam asked.

'I'm guiding them to reach at higher level of consciousness. They seek silence, enlightenment and to be at one with the universe.'

The crowd were all talking.

'Silence. I can help you with this.' Tam jumped up.

'You lot, the big man wants you to shut up, you know, zip it!' he performed the action of pulling a zip across his mouth.

The followers fell silent. He sat down again.

'There you go. So what else are you teaching them?'

'I meant silence from the chattering monkey, not them talking.'

'You're talking about my mum aren't you? Even my dad couldn't stop her yip-yapping. Our only chance would be with a gag.' Tam smiled, pleased with his wisecracks.

'The chattering monkey is not a person but the voice inside your head. I'm here to help these seekers silence that monkey and live in a place of no thought.'

'Drugs, that's the answer. My mother said I had no thought for anyone in those dark days.'

Tam laughed, he was enjoying this meeting and liked the big man. He was kinda cool but could definitely do with a trip to the local gym.

The Buddha closed his eyes.

'So how often do this lot come here?' Tam asked.

'Every day.'

'Slow learners then if they don't get it when you tell them the first time.'

'They are here to find the path towards enlightenment, to the truth, Nirvana. For many of them, it can take years to reach that place, while for some it can happen in the here and now.'

'And so you know about this stuff, do you?'

'The more I know, the more I realise that I know nothing.'

'Is that a riddle? Because if you want to hear my truth, I wasn't very good at school.'

'It's not what you learn in school my friend, it's what's in your heart. That what makes you the person you are. Your heart is where truth resides.'

Tam had enough. He felt better after the water and rice and was ready to move on. He liked this lot but he had places to go and things to do. A wasp was bothering him. His new friend raised a hand.

'Do not harm that wasp. Try and understand it. Tell the wasp you love and respect it, and it will fly away.'

Tam watched as the wasp kept buzzing him. He talked out loud. 'Little wasp, I'm not keen on you and I know this sounds stupid but I love and respect you.'

As he finished his sentence the wasp landed on the back of his hand and jabbed its sting into him twice.

He screamed out loud. 'Bloody hell that was sore. I'm going to kill that wee bugger.'

'And what will that achieve?'

'A wasp free zone.'

He picked the small sting sack out of the back of his hand. An older woman came forward and rubbed ointment on his hand. She wrapped a bandage on his sting.

'I'm Margaret,'

'That's funny, that's my mum's name. Not a name I expected out here from a woman monk.'

'I've only just arrived.'

Tam dug his elbow into the Buddha's ribs. 'Tell me buddy, can you teach me this enlightenment thing.'

'There's nothing to teach. It's there for all. It's right in front of your nose. If you want it- all you have to do is live in the present moment and take it.'

Tam looked and saw the light getting brighter. His breathing wasn't as loud anymore, it fell silent. He looked at the woman Margaret.

'I think this enlightenment thing is happening to me. I'm seeing the light.'

'Go towards it.'

6

BIG TAM'S SPIRITUAL ADVENTURE (PART TWO)

MAGGIE LEFT EARLY BEFORE THE DAILY SUPPLIES ARRIVED AT THE shops below her. Her apartment was two floors above the local traders and she needed to get out before the smell of raw fish and other food would waft up towards her room. She was sure a lot of the food was rotten. She watched in disbelief as mothers regularly bought food from these stalls which lay in the heat most of the day.

She locked her door and made her way along the street dodging the debris in her path.

'Filthy buggers,' she thought as she stepped over what looked like human waste.

She waited on the never-ending stream of traffic to pass.

Mopeds and tuk-tuks were the real danger. She was careful knowing these people didn't value human life as they did back home. She chose her moment and ran crossing in front of a man guiding a cow stacked with bundles of straw.

When she first arrived, she'd watch a cow like this making its way through the traffic. But now she was tired of the setting and wanted nothing more than to be on a flight back home to Castlemilk. Nothing in this strange world seemed to catch her attention anymore.

She made her way into the large modern building that had been her sanctuary and prison for the past nine months. She climbed the three flights of stairs, exhausted.

'Morning Tommy, time to get up.' She walked to the window and threw it open. A breeze as warm as an oven flowed in.

'Tommy boy, are you listening to me? Remember we have a big day ahead of us. I need you to start moving.'

Tommy lay still, his breathing heavy.

'C'mon son, talk to mum.'

She tidied his room arranging his clean pyjamas into his bedside cabinet.

'I'm away to get some towels and a basin.'

She walked the corridor aware that people who usually greeted her were avoiding eye contact.

They know, she thought.

'Time to get your shower. C'mon son, I'm not joking.'

She lifted back the sheets at the bottom of his bed.

'I'm going to take your socks off, it's too hot in here for them. She peeled the cotton socks off and laid them at the bottom of the bed. Wetting her cloth, she went through her daily routine and washed his feet. She rocked his legs from side to side, but they didn't react.

'What's this?' She pulled a grain of rice off the sole of his foot.

'How the hell did that get there? I hope it wasn't bothering you?'

With cotton balls, she washed between each toe and dried them with a towel. She pressed her knuckles into the soles of his feet massaging hard.

'C'mon Tommy, talk to me. I can't help you if you don't help yourself.'

She finished by rubbing massage oil into his feet.

'Your toenails are disgusting and need cut. I'll bring the nail-clippers tomorrow.'

She took a letter from her bag and read it for the fourth time that morning. She tried to hold back the tears.

'Smell this son. If your dad were here he'd call it a bit nancy, but I like it. It's one of the few things about this place I like. The variety of oils.'

Maggie put a small jar filled with amber liquid under his nose.

'Can you smell it son? I like it.'

She took a cloth and washed under his arms and his chest.

She sprayed some scent. You smell better now son. It was definitely a bit iffy when I came in earlier.'

She swung the lamp from above his head and placed her palm on his forehead.

'Jeez, you're burning up. She turned on the fan on the bedside cabinet and held it to his face. This should make you feel like you're back in Scotland with a wee breeze.'

A spray bottle filled with water sat on the table. She squeezed the lever the droplets hopping onto the current of air forming a fine mist on his face. She kept spraying until he felt cool.

She fetched an ice cube from her flask placing it in her hankie. She rubbed the ice on her son's lips the rest melting into slowly into his mouth.

'I know they've stopped giving you fluids, but I won't. Cruel bastards, the lot of them.'

She let more water drip into his mouth.

'I forgot to say I've got a surprise for you. I found something in the wee Indian shop around the corner from my flat that you are going to love. You won't believe me when I tell you. Sitting on the shelf in the fridge was a small pot of creamed rice. Ambrosia. Can you believe that? Ambrosia rice here in the middle of nowhere. I've only ever seen these small pots in the big Asda at Govan.'

She peeled the foil top off and dipped her finger in.

'Oh my God. This is so good, heaven in a plastic pot. Thank God they've not managed to add any spices to it, yet!'

She closed her eyes savouring the taste of something normal from back home. She licked her fingers, one at a time.

'Oh Tommy, if this doesn't wake you up, nothing will.'

She put some rice on her fingers and held it under his nose.

He didn't move, the ventilator breathed in and out for him.

'You must be starving? I tried to stop them turning off your feeding tubes, and now they've done the same with your fluids. I've not abandoned you, I promise. You know I wouldn't give up on you, don't you?'

She looked around before placing her fingers covered in creamed rice into his mouth.

'Here son, try this, we're not supposed to, but who cares?'

She put more into his mouth and melted another ice cube. She wiped his face.

'We don't want to leave the evidence all over your face, do we?

A young nurse walked in and looked at the displays. She flicked her finger against the drip and watched the flow.

'The doctor will be here to see you in thirty minutes, Mrs Donnelly. He asked if you had brought your paperwork?'

Maggie nodded.

'I'd like to appeal and ask for a delay on this decision.'

'YAny changes must be made with the Doctor. I know very little about these things.'

The nurse left the room.

'Right Tommy, it's wake up time.'

She pulled back his eyelids shining the light in from the lamp, his pupils didn't respond.

'Tommy I called Doctor Gupta back home and asked him to call the doctors here. He's one of them so they should understand each other. I don't have a clue what they are all talking about. It's too technical. I asked Gupta to keep your machine on for another while.

Tommy's chest moved up and down the machine feeding a steady flow of oxygen to his body./p> She tapped him on the head.

''Tommy, I know you're in there, talk to me. Have you any idea about what they are going to do to you today? Give me a small sign, anything.'

She looked at his vacant eyes, nothing. She whispered in his ear.

'I've never told you this before son, at least not the way a mum should. You sort of know what I'm going to tell you. I love you, and I need you. I can't carry on with life if you leave me.'

''Tommy!' She shook him roughly.

A doctor and two nurses entered the room. Maggie sat back on her chair. The doctor looked at the displays and wrote down some notes.

'Take a seat, Mrs Donnelly. You know where we are today and what we have to do. Don't you?'

'Doctor, I want to ask for an extension. Another three months if that's possible. I'm positive my Tommy's going to wake up at any moment. He nods and winks and moves his eyebrows to me all the time when I speak to him. He'll wake up soon, I know he will.'

'Mrs Donnelly, nine months have passed since the motorbike hit your son. His injuries were so severe we've seen no brain activity since. You are the only one who says he signals to you when we know it isn't the case. The court has already ruled on the cruelty of keeping him alive in this vegetative state.

'And who's looking for the criminal on the motorbike? No one.'

'Please Mrs Donnelly, that's a police matter. As you know, this week under instruction from the court we removed Thomas's fluids and feeding tube. He's already weakened by this. The only thing keeping him alive is the ventilator. It's time we switched it off for both you and Thomas' sake.'

'Please don't. I'm begging you doctor, give me a little more time. A few days. I need to spend more time with him. He's my son, the only thing I've got left in this world.'

'I'm sorry Mrs Donnelly, it's today.'

'Didn't you talk to Dr Gupta? Didn't he tell you about Tommy?'

'He did. He mentioned he was a fine character and very funny. He felt sad as he only knew him for his heroin addiction. But he said he was a good man who was very much loved by you.'

'That's true and why I have to protect him.'

'Can you call your family back home?'

'I don't have any, well except some bad ones that I wouldn't talk to. I'm afraid it was only Tommy, me and his dad Sandy and he died three years ago.'

'Mrs Donnelly, I have an instruction from the high court to turn off his machine today. I have no choice. What if I give you another hour with him to say your goodbyes. You can lie up beside him if you want and we'll put the curtain round if you want to give your boy a cuddle.'

The doctor put his hand on her arm. 'You know it's time.'

Maggie looked at him tears dripping off her face. She nodded.

'Can you sign this letter please, it's the same as the one you have.'

Maggie took the pen in her hands, shaking. She focused on the words... AGREE TO TURN OF THE LIFE SUPPORT VENTILATOR. She scribbled on the paper her signature looking nothing like it normally does.

The nurses ran the curtain around the bed and pulled Tommy over to one side.

'You can lie here beside your son, I'll be back at noon. I'll give him a little something to settle him before we switch off the machine. Make sure you tell him everything you want to while you can. Don't have any regrets later on. Tell him to head towards the light.'

The doctor left the room.

Maggie swatted away a few flies that were around Tommy's face.

'Bloody flies. We won't miss you. She swatted a couple with her cloth and hit Tommy on the arm.

'Sorry Tommy, I didn't mean that.'

She could see one of the nurses had positioned herself on a chair outside the curtain.

She must be there to make sure I don't try and run off with Tommy's bed, she thought.

She climbed onto the bed and hugged her son. She whispered in his ear.

'I'm going to hurt you but it's for your own good. I need to waken you. This may save you. She took a small lapel badge off her blouse and opened it exposing the sharp pin. She took his hand in hers.

'Sorry son, but you'll thank me later.'

She pushed the pin into the back of his hand drawing blood. She watched the monitors for reaction, nothing not even a blimp. She pulled the pin out and stuck it in again, further still with no reaction.

'That was my last hope Tommy. I thought you'd jump up.'

She put her arm around him and cuddled up to him. She drifted back thinking of the crazy times they'd spent together. They never had money but they laughed so much. She remembered keeping him up late to watch the old black and white movies into the early hours. He knew all the stars from that time.

And then it was the Hammer Horror movies, which scared them both while his dad lay drunk on the couch.

She remembered when he changed, following his father drinking alcohol. This led to smoking cannabis which took him to heroin. By then it was too late.

She remembered how she lost him back then. The wilderness years. She always loved him no matter and now she was losing him for the second time.

She was so proud when he turned himself around and became sober. Everyone said it wasn't possible, but Tommy proved them wrong. No drink, no drugs and he even kicked smoking. Two years he was off it all because he'd met some monks on the streets of Glasgow. He attended their meetings and seemed so happy in that time. He even got a job, a first for the family.

And then this big announcement. A spiritual journey to India.

'I'll be back in six months mum, she remembered. I'll talk to you every day, I promise.'

'India son, what the hell's in India.'

'Meditation, peace, a journey. Everything I want. It will be life-changing.'

She looked at him and kissed his cheek. Tears flowed.

She remembered the knock on her door.

'Your son has been in an accident, he's critical.'

Life changing right enough. The street did a fundraiser through social media. They raised enough money for a flight and accommodation for a few months. She wondered how she managed to survive and do everything herself for the past nine months. But she had.

'Tommy, it's decision time. I'm going with you. I want to be with you and your dad. I can't watch you die or be responsible for turning off your life after giving it to you in the first place. I would rather be with you in heaven.'

She kissed her son on the cheek and pulled the hose aside and then on the lips.

She reached into her pocket and pulled out his pocket knife. It was one of the few things he had with him at the time of his accident.

'Love you always son.'

She twisted the bedsheet and filled her mouth with the material to stifle her scream. She pushed the knife blade hard into her wrist, pulling it back and forth and twisting. She bit hard trying not to make a noise. She managed to cut through the main vein and could feel her wrist warm pumping large amounts of blood onto the bed.

She cleared her mouth and cuddled up against her son, smiling.

''Tommy I never said it to you in thirty-five years and now I can't stop. I love you my beautiful boy. I love you so much. Thank you for being a wonderful son. I hope I was a good mother.'

She shivered as she lay on the bed.

''Tommy, I think the doctor was correct, I can see a bright light. Go towards the light.'

The pool of blood spread across the bed soaking her and Tommy.

'Love you.' she said.

7

GOING DOWN THE TOWN

I REMEMBER WHEN 'GOING DOWN THE TOWN' WAS A REGULAR thing. At fourteen years old, I would meet my mother every Friday after school to help her with the weekly shopping at Tesco's. Between us we carried a dozen or more heavy shopping bags filled with potatoes, milk and a bevy of tins.

The memory of us struggling to carry these bags remains etched in my brain. We had to stop so many times to give our hands some relief from the weight and the plastic handles that stretched under the strain, cutting off the circulation in our hands.

The bus terminus in Greenock oozed a dank smell that never seemed to shift from the filthy concrete structure. It was always wet and cold standing in line trying to see the arriving buses through frosted glass windows. This always puzzled me as the one thing everyone needs at a bus station is to see which buses are arriving. The stupidity of the glass meant people had to walk back and forth to look through the exposed gaps to see which buses were arriving.

Hard-working people filled the queues, and from their faces it was clear many were struggling with everyday life. They waited patiently, not knowing if they would get on the approaching bus. It was hard to know if the bus would arrive empty or full to the brim.

Reading was my passion and as I stood in amongst the crowd, I remembered a quote I'd read. It said, 'Although people struggle with poverty they are usually happy within'. Looking at the faces surrounding me I found this hard to believe. The people I grew up beside often just wanted the smallest of breaks. A win to uplift their spirits and relieve them from the constant battering that often took them to breaking point.

Our town centre was filthy. Pavements patterned with chewing-gum and litter that people threw on the ground with scant regard. The wind would whip up the loose rubbish into mini tornadoes, sending it flying and giving me something to focus on. I remember a woman in a queue next to me saying, 'If we put the rubbish in the bins, then the street cleaners will be out of a job.' This was part of the mentality back then.

Cigarette butts were thick on the ground and the smell of dampness and nicotine from people's clothes would make me retch. There was some solace from the sounds echoing up from the nearby underpass. A one legged man would play his clarinet for hours propped against the wall with his crutch. He was a talented musician and the first real busker I had come across. His missing leg was fascinating to me and for years I wanted to ask what happened to it but stern words from my mother meant I never found out. His music would take me off from the misery of my situation to some dream state when he played 'Strangers on the Shore'.

Every week I questioned why it was me in the queue. How come my brothers and sister sidestepped this chore, each claiming it was my job because I was the youngest. It always felt unfair, but someone had to help.

Wherever you find crowds of people, you inevitably get 'chancers' and this bus terminus was no different. There were always someone looking for opportunities and in Greenock they gravitated from three places. The pub, the bookies or the amusement arcades. These guys would stand in shop doorways, ferret-like searching the faces of the 'tired commuters' looking for some unwilling victim. They would throw their betting slips away, leaving them more desperate at returning home with no wages. Fags with an inch of grey ash would hang from their mouths ready to fall onto their less than clean shirts. In need of money they would target the people at the bus queues trying to cadge money from people who were already broke.

The approach rarely changed and they would walk up and down the queues knowing it was a new audience every twenty or thirty minutes. 'Hello hen, I've lost my bus fare home - any chance I could borrow ten pence from you? or 'there's a dead cert on the three o'clock at Chepstow - lend me fifty pence and I'll double your money before you get on the bus.'

My mother was used to dealing with men, having worked in Kincaid's, the local shipyard canteen. She spotted these guys coming at us long before I'd notice them. She would mutter under her breath - 'here we go' a sign something was about to kick off.

With a steely eyed glare and her voice raised a few extra decibels she would scream as they approached, 'Piss Off. Go earn your own money'. I was sure some guy would smack her but it seemed to work as the poor sod who made the approach would make a hasty retreat and avoid this 'not officially diagnosed, but easy to recognise', mad woman. I would stare at the ground avoiding eye contact with those around me who must have thought she'd lost it, but no one seemed to bother. I think secretly they were pleased someone stood up to these beggars.

The rain would pour down and a gaggle of grannies would reach into their bags for the simplest invention of that time. They would unfold a small square of polythene into three before unfolding it further and tying two cotton ribbons around their chin. The rainmate was born - a simple way of keeping their hair dry even though half of them were wearing curlers out in public.

As the bus pulled up, the people onboard couldn't get off because the queue was trying to push its way on. In any other country you enter and leave at different ends of the vehicle, but not here. We had a steel pole in the middle of the entrance which had no rules associated with it and so passengers tried to push past on both sides creating the odd bit of aggravation. As if life wasn't bad enough travelling by bus, my mother made it far worse by insisting on going upstairs for a smoke.

With our bags feeling heavier and almost at a breaking point, we would push on up the small twisting staircase. If we were lucky, there would be an empty seat, but most times the bus was full. Standing never bothered my mum as long as she could light her cigarette and drag on that thick blue smoke. A dozen other smokers puffed away, collectively creating an unnatural fog for everyone else to choke on. I used to hope that one sensible person would open a window, but they rarely did.

My mother would search though her bags looking for the new catalogue given to her at the checkout. This was the era of Green Shield stamps which each shopper received with every purchase. I remember the checkout girl pressing a small button and the machine would spill out a waterfall of stamps that seemed never-ending. I knew I wouldn't be licking them.

My mother had collected a pile of these floppy stamp books and would constantly quote how many stamps an item was worth.

'480 stamps and we can get a toaster - no more sticking it under the grill,' she would say.

She ignored my question if we could put cheese and pickle in a toaster. She was onto another page of her latest catalogue.

'We've enough for a sleeping bag or if we save 1200 stamps, we can get a 'Teas Maid'. Listen to this - the Teas Maid will wake us in the morning with an alarm call and a hot cup of tea - I don't think any of our neighbours will have one of those.'

Apart from the supermarket stamps she also saved the coupons from her Player's No.6 cigarettes. The one guarantee with all these stamps and coupons was we always ended up with some crappy item that we would never use.

Our cupboards overflowed with crap, K-tel record selectors, drinks glasses, magic mops to clean the lino and brush-o-matics to take the fluff off our clothes. I could already see the Teas Maid being set up and used for three of four days then she would forget to add the water or milk at night or clean it and it would mould away before being relegated to the hall cupboard with all the other junk.

The bus conductress broke my dream state as she made her way along the aisle jingling her money. She stood in front of us. It was an art watching my mother trying to pay our fares while placing her bags on the floor without them toppling over. She searched through her pockets, no money just some half-smoked doubts and a polo mint. Her pockets were always disgusting.

'One and a half to Ratho Street' she said.

'What age is he?' asked the conductress, pointing at me as if I was some kind of mute.

'Twelve,' we both said together. Our well-rehearsed reply had finally worked. He's big for his age…' my mother would start to justify.

'I think he's been twelve for the last three years,' the clippie muttered under her breath while deftly performing a concertina movement with around twenty coins making a beautiful rattling sound. I watched as she wound the small handle on her ticket machine twice, the noise from the ratchet followed by the appearance of two small lavender tickets. She tore them off and handed them to me.

We finally got a seat, and I leaned against the window to get a nap. The vibration from the old diesel engine juddered my head so much my face felt like rubber, leaving me slightly woozy. Ten minutes later, I pressed the button on the ceiling to give the driver enough warning. The worst possibility when carrying this many bags would be to miss our stop. We squeezed past the other passengers, headed downstairs and got off at the big crane on the main road. Ratho Street was steep, but it felt more like climbing a mountain with the weight of our bags.

Struggling and out of breath, my mother's cigarette remained in her mouth even as she choked from her weekly exertion. She placed her bags down to catch her breath. I could have guessed what was about to happen. A large brown potato spilled from her bag and ran for its life. It rolled down the hill in an uneven and strange side-to-side motion. One by one, its fellow potatoes followed in hot pursuit, all rolling in that same uneven wobbly way past my feet. I tried to catch them, but there were too many heading in multiple directions. My mother put down her bags and chased after them just as some apples and tangerines made a run for it too. It was the 'Great Escape' of the fruit and veg world who must have realised their fate in the coming week.

My arms were too tired by now and I laid my bags on top of my mother's stopping any more items from spilling out. A neighbour walked out of our close, dressed in what looked like a new black leather jacket. He was too smooth for this area. He nodded to me; but no offer of help.

I stared down the street where my mum had an armful of

potatoes and apples and a small pile of orange shapes gathered at her feet. Each time she picked one up, another would fall, she should've taken a bag with her. The neighbour stopped and picked up the tangerines. He was putting them all into my mum's pockets. With both hands in her jacket pockets and her arms full he pulled her towards him his face inches from hers. They stared at each other before my mother nodded towards me. He turned and looked, whispered something to her then walked away, throwing his arms in the air as he left. She struggled up the street out of breath.

'What was that about?' I asked.

'What are you talking about? He was helping me with the fruit and veg. If you know what's best for you, you'll keep it buttoned. Wait here till I drop these home then come back for you.'

She headed up the stairs to the first landing, the potatoes and apples balanced in her arms. I heard a commotion and then swearing echoing down the stairs and out onto the street. Someone was getting an earful. She came back her face red, my dad following behind looking sheepish.

'Do you know what your father just asked me while my arms were full and I strained to rap that stupid heavy letterbox with my nose?'

I shook my head.

'Tell him,' she shouted.

I looked at my dad his arms splayed in his usual dramatic way; a pretend hurt look on his face.

'What? he said. I only asked what was for dinner tonight.'

8

A CRESCENT MOON

A crescent moon on a winter's night sky
made me smile
Clouds rush by illuminated, like ships heading to new
lands
A fox, stands still in the shadows, observing the street
It's bigger than the usual ones we see around here
sniffing the night air and catching scents that take a free
ride on the light breeze
On tip toes the fox moves swiftly, disappearing silently
through a neighbour's hedge

Her search for food on these cold nights, intensifies
while her cubs obey, curled up in a hole with neither
sound nor movement.

9

OLD FRIENDS

Every day, Death rides towards us,
emotionless in her quest
We all see her in the distance and yet
we close our eyes,
but she'll never go away or yield to our requests

While Life, she stretches out before us
welcoming with every breath,
compelling us to demand far more
from the confines of the time we've left

Know that a meeting of these oldest of friends
is never far away
They'll fight hard for you as they both engage
It's just a role they have to play

Take each breath and make it count

10

A MOGGY'S TALE

Tikka sleeping on windowsill
Tail flicking, in midday sun
Ears twist towards every sound
as a bee buzzes along the ground

Whiskers twitch as dreams abound
Belly full, gentle snoring sounds
Little pink tongue just poking out
It's a cat's life, without a doubt

11

MOTHER NATURE'S TEARS

I plucked the moon from the beautiful night sky
My heart raced fast as light shone in my eyes
A silvery finger touched me deep in my dreams
Mother Nature was dying, pollution, it seems

I leaned over closer and in her last dying breath
She said I've failed all you people, your destination's now death
I grabbed and I shook her, please don't leave us to die
She stopped, somewhat shocked, with tears in her eyes

She said it's too late to save the world when few
people care
They all want their comforts, they'll not take the stairs
This laziness, your downfall, of our planet, once fantastic
Ruined by man's own pollution, that scourge you call
plastic

Is there something I can do to help Earth become better?
Not now, with icebergs melting, your land's going to get
wetter
Those corporates who abuse power, with only profits in
sight
They turn and they look away, knowing fine well it's not
right

My glaciers are melting, my rainforests are being felled
My oceans are being choked and the wildlife's being killed
For people's strawberry tarts, presented in plastic so clear
A few minutes to eat them, landfill waste for many years

I'll help you to reverse this to stop this world getting
worse
You don't get it, it's too late, your pollution's a curse
But I could start a campaign, help people become
awakened
Then teach them to respect earth, or we'll all be forsaken

I was shocked Mother Nature, was this messenger
of doom
Her words struck dark fear with her foreboding gloom
I pleaded, please rescue us, from this last chance saloon
She said I've not told you the worst yet, some idiot stole
the moon

12

COMFY PANTS

BLOSSOM, A MIDDLE-AGED, WELL-ROUNDED FAIRY HID UNDER THE flute of a daffodil that was bent over with the weight of the torrential rain. Her face lit up like the sun from the yellow glow surrounding her. She peeked out, watching as the rain poured down, creating small rivulets across the forest floor.

Her hiding place was uncomfortable, squashed for a long period inside the flower's trumpet and to make matters worse her knicker elastic was cutting into her cheeks.

'Must buy bigger pants, she said out loud, or perhaps make a pair with some magic.'

She looked at her wand, and then at the size of her problem. 'Hmm not enough fairy dust left to cast a spell that powerful.'

The rain was relentless and began seeping under her hideaway. Sitting up she pulled her toes in further to avoid her feet getting soaked.

She watched large raindrops run down the daffodil before dripping off the rim onto the ground. Trying to amuse herself she decided to lie underneath and catch a drip in her mouth. She followed a raindrop as it wound its way downwards towards the edge, shuffling her body over she lined up her mouth to catch the cool refreshment. The drop held on for ages stretching slowly to a teardrop shape. She opened her mouth as wide as possible, just as the drip sprung free falling towards her mouth in slow motion. Her eyes were wide in anticipation and then plop, the drip missed her mouth, hitting her square on the forehead. She let out a scream.

Laughter rang out from someone nearby. She pulled up the yellow silky curtain and looked across to see Bluebell hiding beneath a large fern. She was a mischievous fairy who lived far beyond the big tree.

'What are you doing Blossom? You're losing it.'

Blossom grinned. "Sorry, she said in a high-pitched voice, didn't know anyone was watching me.'

A cheer arose in the forest. From under tree roots, snowdrops and other plants at least twelve other fairies appeared clapping their hands.

'Take a bow Missy Blossom, you know how to make a rainy day more fun,' shouted Starlight.

Blossom's face turned red. She had a thing for him and couldn't help admire how hot he looked in his purple fairy tight leggings.

'A girl can always dream,' she whispered to herself, smiling and curling up under her yellow rain cover.

A long low rumble thundered overhead bringing yet another

downpour. The magic circle was soon deserted as the fairies disappeared back into their hiding places.

A swirl of fairy dust as bright as the stars appeared from under the bottom of a tree. Twinkling, the dust danced and twinkled as it made its way across the forest floor heading towards the daffodil. The magic dust slipped with ease under the flute before surrounding Blossom. She felt giddy when she recognised her surprise had been sent from Starlight.

She took her wand, waving gently, wondering what he'd sent her.

The dust gathered itself into a ball changing shape as the middle-aged fairy watched with excitement. The magic dust transformed into a handbag, she smiled 'a girl can never have too many of these,' she thought looking at it. She decided to let it go. The dust quickly turned into a toadstool, 'no! definitely not, she said, been there and done that.' She watched as the glittering dust shaped itself into a large pair of pants. Blossom sat back and smiled. She ran her wand through silvery pants, accepting the gift. The daffodil flute burst into a kaleidoscope of colour as the dust worked its magic firing light off in every direction.

Blossom let out a sigh of relief.

'Oh my, she said flapping her large loose pants, comfort at last. How I love rainy afternoons.'

13
GLASGOW

I like Glasgow best
more real than our somewhat fake capital
I love sitting at the concert hall steps
Watching people, watch people

There are a few bumpers out today
Glaikit some would say
While unfortunates lie penniless in doorways
And buskers entertain

A magnificent view down Buchanan Street
Throngs of people on the move

Branded shopping bags, today's badges of honour
Filled with short-lived satisfaction

But it's the patter that cheered me up today
"Hey Aggie ya effin boot"
"Aw howsit going Mary"
As they hug, insult, not understood

© Grahame Anderson Storyteller - May 12th 2019

14

SMILE

A girl I once knew never smiled
She tried terribly hard for a while
Then she met a young guy
Who stared deep in her eyes
Now you can see her smile from a mile

15

THE GALVI BUCKET

GILLIAN LAY HER HEAD BACK AGAINST THE WINDOW FRAME AND blew a long stream of smoke into the air. With one leg jammed against the bricks, her other leg hung outside the window swinging back and forth. She wasn't in a good place. Her phone buzzed interrupting her train of thought. She glanced at the message on the screen.

"I'm watching you."

She looked across to her boyfriend's house and sees Jack standing at the window scratching his bare chest. He waves to her.

She types a quick reply, her long nails getting in the way.

"Leave me alone. I'm thinking," She takes another drag from her cigarette.

"Should you be smoking?" he messages her

"Really Jack, is that the best you can say to me right now?"

"I'm only thinking about your current situation."

"Go away. I don't need reminding from you."

Her mother shouts from downstairs.

"Gillian! Get yourself down here, now! I need help."

Gillian rubbed the tip of her cigarette back and forth against the roughcast wall and placed the half-smoked cigarette back in its packet. Too expensive to waste, she thought.

"Gillian! Did you hear me?"

She climbed back into her room spraying perfume to cover the smell of smoke.

"What now?" she muttered.

In the kitchen, her mother is standing next to the sink.

"Watch this. she said and turns on the tap. Muddy brown water flows into the white ceramic bowl.

"I forgot they were working on the water pipes today, - I can't cook or wash in this filth."

"What do you want me to do about it?"

"Take those two buckets and fill them for me. The council have placed a bowser at the top of the street for the next forty-eight hours."

"A what?"

"A bowser. A big tank full of fresh water. Fill the buckets and bring them back. Don't take too long if you want dinner."

"Sorry mum, I'm heading out."

"You're going nowhere till you get me water. If you so much as think of going out..."

"What is it with you mum?"

"Me! What's got into you lately? Go and fetch the water and

change those jeans. You're not walking the streets with the knees out of them, they look ridiculous."

"It's called fashion mum, but you wouldn't get it."

"Gillian! Just get the water."

"And how will I carry two buckets by myself?"

"You have two arms."

"And what kind of bucket is this anyway, it's minging." She held up a grey steel bucket in the air.

"It's a galvi bucket. Don't they teach you anything useful at school?"

"Well, I must have missed my history lesson when Hitler gave everyone in the German army a galvi bucket. Jeez, how stupid am I?"

"You're getting far too cheeky Gillian. I should visit your school and hear what the teachers say about you and your backchat."

"They care as much about me as I do for them."

"Call lover boy and tell him to get over here and help you. He's got to be useful for something."

Gillian didn't want to get into an argument with her mother about Jack. She knew her mother didn't like him and there was no point in defending him in front of her. She texted him to come over.

"What for?" he replied.

"Never mind, get over here pronto."

Five minutes later Jack sauntered in dressed in his jeans and white tee-shirt smiling.

"Hello Mrs T. Looking lovely as ever."

"Don't give me that bull son. Try the fake charm on someone else."

"C'mon, let's go." Gillian pulled at Jack's arm and picked up the buckets.

They stopped in the lane outside her house. Jack pulled her

close to him. “What the hell's up with your mum? said Jack. She's such a moaning cow.”

“Tell me about it. I have to live with her.”

“Have you told her, about you know what?” he placed his hand on her and rubbed her belly. She removed his hand looking around.

“Do you think you would still be alive if I had told her. You’re not thinking straight Jack, I’m fifteen, you’re seventeen. You could face charges for touching a minor as 'technically' you're an adult.”

Jack stared at her somewhat shocked.

“You wouldn't say it was me, would you?”

“Who the hell else would people think it was?”

“Tell your mum someone attacked you on the way home from the club one night and you didn’t want to say.”

Gillian shook her head and wondered about Jack's level of intelligence. “Never mind Jack - you let me think about it. We need to go and get this stupid water.”

They shared a cigarette as they headed up the hill. A queue of people stood in line next to a large blue tank filling buckets and containers of all shapes and colours.

After five minutes it was Jack's turn. He filled the two buckets.

He waddled over to a piece of waste ground overlooking the valley.

"Jeez, this metal bucket is heavy."

"I know and it's disgusting looking. I'm not drinking any of the water that comes out of it."

They sat on an old leather couch someone had fly-tipped onto the piece of wasteland. It was comfy. A few other items were next to the couch including an old fridge and other bits and pieces.

“Take in the view and enjoy it gorgeous,” Jack said putting his arm around her shoulder.

“You won't be calling me gorgeous when I'm as fat as her from number fourteen, will you? Jack I’m trying to stay calm, but I can't think straight for more than ten seconds since I saw the results. My head is churning all day every day. Do you think I should get another kit and test myself again?"

"There's no point. We've done it three times. We can't afford to keep testing. Go to your doctor and see if they can do something?"

"Like what?"

"You know?..." Jack stared at her.

"Don't go there, Jack Wilson. Promise me you won't ever say that again."

Jack looked away. He turned his attention to the rubbish scattered across the piece of waste ground pointing to a lime green shape.

"Look at the plastic sledge Gillian. We could slide down the hill and walk the tracks back to your house."

"I'm not sliding down there. Look how steep it is?"

"C'mon, it will be a laugh, where's all your fun gone. I'll sit at the front and steer, you can hold the buckets on the sledge behind me."

"I'm not doing it Jack. Look at the grass it's all bumpy and there's a small wall at the bottom. Let's head back the way we came."

Jack lifted the plastic sledge and looked disappointed. A large crack ran from one end to the other. He spied a wooden board with a solid frame around it, a local baker's name burned into each side.

"Look at this Gillian, it's perfect."

He dragged the board towards the steep incline and balanced it on the edge of the hill.

"I am not sitting on that thing Jack. There's no way I'm going near that ."

"Don't be daft. It'll be a laugh. Grab a cushion from the old couch."

"You've got to be kidding me. We'll have no water in the buckets when we get to the bottom. You're definitely losing it."

"Okay, I promise if we spill the water I'll pour what we have into one bucket and run back up and get more. C'mon Gillian, let's do it. Live fast, die young, all that sort of stuff."

"Okay, as long as you promise not to go fast."

"Do you think I would be that stupid?"

Gillian shrugged her shoulders. She placed the cushion on the board and sat at the back. She lifted the buckets and placed them beside her. Jack sat up front and shuffled forward.

"We need to throw our weight forward to tip it over the edge to get it moving," They both shuffled forward but the board remained rooted to the same spot. Two boys playing kerbie came over to watch them.

"That looks dangerous," one of them said.

"What are you, some kind of Health and Safety inspector? Just give us a push over the edge."

The two boys looked at each other and laughed. "Are you sure about this?"

"Of course. Go on give us a start."

The two boys pushed hard against the board, it didn't move.

"Push on my girlfriend's back," Jack shouted.

They both leaned against Gillian not sure where to place their hands and pushed again. The board inched forward.

"That's it guys, again," said Jack.

They pushed harder this time with some success moving the board closer to the edge.

"Once more should do it," said Jack.

The boys gave one last shove and the board tipped over with ease and with its passengers it took off down the hill.

Jack whooped and hollered and pushed back against Gillian as their makeshift sledge gained speed. Water from the buckets sloshed onto Gillian's jeans and white tee shirt soaking her. She screamed from the coldness. Jack tried hard to slow the board down with his hands digging hard into the grass but it was impossible. His hand caught on something and he pulled it back and saw blood pouring from a wound. The board bumped and lifted off the ground several times before crashing head-on into a large rock. A horrific noise cut through the air as the board cracked and splintered. Jack slumped forward his face smashing hard against the rock. The galvanised bucket flew forward, the sharp metal rim slicing the top part of his scalp off. Gillian's body continued forward slamming against the back of Jack's head. She felt a sharp pain in her ribs and heard Jack's neck make a snapping sound as her body flew over the top of his.

Her body rolled at full speed and out of control down the hill tumbling head over heels like a rag doll. She flew through the air as she hit off the small wall, landing hard on the large stones at the side of the train tracks. She lay still, battered and bruised.

She looked back up the hill and could see Jack beside the rock. His head was hanging at a strange angle. His body convulsed and then stopped.

Gillian watched as the two young boys came sliding down the hill towards them.

"It wasn't our fault," one said. You told us to push you."

Gillian nodded before passing out.

THE END

THIS IS a simple exercise anyone can do. Take a traditional story or nursery rhyme and make it real. You know the story all you have to do is embellish it. It's obvious my story is Jack and Jill. All I had to go on was the following:

Jack and Jill went up the hill

to fetch a pail of water,
Jack fell down and broke his crown
and Jill came tumbling after.

Try something similar and see how you get on. You could rewrite any story or nursery rhyme. Go on give it a try

16
CONVERSATION STOPPER

As I travelled on the train back from my concert in York this week, at Durham station an older couple came onboard and sat beside me.

They were from South Africa on a month-long religious pilgrimage. They told me their itinerary included visits to Scotland and Israel.

Thinking this could be interesting and always looking for topics to write about I got chatting to them.

I asked where they were going to in Scotland thinking maybe Iona Abbey which I know sees thousands of pilgrims each year.

'Motherwell', said the woman.

'What's in Motherwell?' I ask.

'A minister', she said. 'He is the only person who speaks with the authority of God as his words were meant to be spoken.'

'Yikes! I thought, What little I knew about this world and Motherwell.'

'I never knew there was someone that important in Motherwell,' I said. 'Is this minister on the world stage?' I asked.

'He is the only one with authority.' she said again.

As diplomatic as I am, I changed the conversation. I asked if she had seen the funny story the previous week about the minister who asked his followers to donate $54 million so he could buy a new plane - his selling line was 'if Jesus was here he would want one and not travel about on a donkey.'

They both stared at me

Anyway, I thought it was funny.

She remained stoic then shook her head. She hadn't seen it and for some reason unknown to me, she wasn't taking the conversation forward. Another problem I have is talking about things I know nothing about. The Israel/Palestine conflict is a good example.. I know nothing about it and I don't know which side is which and who I'm meant to be supporting if any of them.

As she said she was going to Israel I thought I would give it a mention, - obviously, now 24 hours after having this conversation I realise maybe it wasn't such a good idea! All I knew about the conflict is what I had seen on TV a few night previously. So I opened my big mouth.

'It's terrible all the young Palestinian people getting shot when you consider all these people are meant to believe in God. You think they could work it out and live in harmony.'

Stoney silence - Paddington hard stare.

'I'm just thinking of the young men and women being shot and killed. That's not right to anyone with a Christian belief.' I said.

'Genesis 6:5' - she murmured.

'Sorry I'm not up to date with my verse numbers.'

She said and I quote - 'We all have a terrible wickedness in our hearts and all are totally evil.'

Conversation stopper.

My turn to give the stoney stare of disbelief.

She continued. 'If any good is done it is not because of humans. It is only because God allows it.'

Did I just hear that in 2018?

I decided not to go there as much as I would have loved to, but I'm sitting on a crowded train and I was trying to do the right thing by welcoming them to Scotland.

Change the conversation I thought.

I mention I went to see the Dalai Lama a few years back and how he gave a wonderful talk about the people of the world.

Another faux pas - wry smile - almost smug at the mention of HH Dalai Lama.

I continued unfazed, purposely by saying -

'His Holiness said, there's a family in India in a modest house and the parents would like a little more money, more education and good health in the coming year. Also, in a favela in Brazil, there's a single mother and she would like a little more money, more education and good health in the coming year for her and her daughter. In Iraq the same and in fact in most communities across the world, this is the simple dream of most of the world's population. Just to have things a little better each year and to have less trouble in the world.

The Dalia Lama reminded the audience whether Christian, Muslim, Sikh, Buddhist, whatever, the majority wanted these simple things. Only a small part of one per cent of people was troubled and wanted to harm others and had few morals.

As I relayed this wonderful little story it was not taken onboard. I think thoughts of wickedness abounded towards me.

We continued our four-hour journey with small talk about

the weather thinking it was probably best to avoid the big items. Just as well really as outside storm clouds were building in the sky and I'm sure a few bolts of lightning were lining up for me.

As the good atheist that I am (please note: an atheist does not mean - a person devoid of morals) I helped them off the train and carried their bags for them, shaking hands and genuinely wishing them well on their pilgrimage and in life. I guess the wickedness hasn't got me that much or maybe I only helped them because God allowed me too.

Anyway, every day's a school day and each to their own.

If you don't talk to people and ask them questions you don't learn new things. I enjoyed it as an experience and learnt there are people in the world who think very differently from me.

Enjoy life, help others and try not to think about wickedness and evil in your heart. It's not to be believed. Remember the human race is inherently good.

17
THE EDGE OF REALITY

I need sleep, eyes are tired, they strain to keep open
Can't stay awake, I struggle, I'm not sure I'm coping
The abyss, I welcome, fall headlong to my dreams
and Morpheus, he leads me, to a place of extremes

Cocooned and cosy under the weight of my covers
I let the day go, no doubt, they'll be others
Slipping silently into, a curious world of dreams
As numbness surrounds me, I fly off on moonbeams

To the sky, floating upwards, I climb at great speed
Astral travelling can be fun or is this part of my dream
I glide over mountains, with golden eagles I soar
Then I fall like a feather, spiral down, I'm no more

Intoxicating fragrance fills my head to the brim
Feeling high on these perfumes, I float around my room
The light from the sun feeds the garden, gives a glow
Then my spirit rises up, different dreams, another show

Symphonic music, notes flutter through the air
Vibrations of sound bring thoughts of yesteryear
I sit on God's couch, drinking tea in her tent
My request is for love, with war we're all spent

I travel through forests, the oceans and space
Looking down on Earth I question our human race
Will we get it together, treat others with grace
Maybe, one day, we just might find that place

Coming back, from my dream, I recoil into my self
This body I travel in, a true picture of health ;0)
My eyes barely open, did I manage some sleep?
I 'm not feeling better, it couldn't have been deep

18

THE KITCHEN TABLE

Ten years to this day, we became adult orphans
The passing of my mother was a hard blow to take
We gathered around her table, where each day we ate
The effect on our lives wasn't quite realised yet

To lose your parents, nothing much worse can happen
The loss of their wisdom, cheerleading and clapping
Our parents were our strength, as we developed and grew
They knew when to speak, and when to challenge our
views

Their home is long gone, all that's left is our memories
Of when our family all gathered to share big pots of soup
Aunts, Uncles and cousins, and hungry kids from our
street
Would get their fill at our table and some ate like pigs

Our kitchen table was central to our challenging lives
It witnessed our dramas, four generations, across time
It's where everyone would talk, sort problems, pull
together
And when the talking was done, somehow we all felt
better

In the mornings we'd start with a steaming bowl of
porridge
At lunch, we'd have soup, usually lentil of course
Big chunks of bread and always a thick wedge of butter
Everyone was fed, but always last was my mother

The adults would argue and be deep in discussion
Today it was about Billy, our daft, wayward cousin
He'd taken someone's car and crashed into a field
He denied it was him, but his eyes couldn't conceal

We sat there in silence the time our grandad had died
We were all dressed in black, men and women both cried
He was a character, a worker, smoking twenty a day
A whisky each night then for his family he'd pray

Gran's in the kitchen with her plates and her pots
She can always make a meal from not a hell of a lot
No pre-made sauces or quick four-minute meals
It'd be potatoes, leeks, onions and carrots, hand peeled

My memories of our home are of the meeting of people
Now families don't do that, why not, aren't we able?
Everyone's busy and they all live miles apart
And no one seems bothered to lose a home with a heart

So what's with the table, a piece of wood with a cover
It brought love to our family and a place to discover
A focal point we shared, breaking bread, welcoming others
Our kitchen, our table, our family, our mother.

19

FUNNY OLD MOON

The Moon is falling towards our skies
At massive speed and we don't know why
I hope it sinks at sea and avoids our land
Will its light go out, will we lose the man

The moon is falling and it's not a lie
Can we push it back, push it way up high
With rockets and ropes, we could give it a try
To stop it crashing through our bright blue sky

We'd miss our moon if we had an empty sky
Nowhere for lovers promising do or die
A sky full of darkness, shooting stars that zoom
I'd much rather we kept our funny old moon.

20
MACINTOSH THE DOG – PART 1

THE FIRST DAY

I REMEMBER the day Brenda and I headed to the dog rescue centre in Glasgow. We'd decided it was time to get ourselves a pup and our excitement was spilling over. We drove to the city with the cardboard box we had prepared and lined with a furry blanket. A comfy first start for the Labrador pup we wanted.

We received our pep talk from the staff and told the woman it had to be a labrador. She suggested we walk through the cages and 'see what we see'. 'Everyone wants a pup, she said. The older dogs if not picked have a poor chance of survival.' Her words were startling.

We notice the old boys and girls who've been given in: perhaps their owners suffered from ill health or passed away. There's fear in these old dogs' eyes. They've come from years in a safe home with a comfortable sofa or favourite rug in front of the fire. Now they're lying on a concrete floor next to cages full of nervous pups barking, whining and trying to get out.

We passed through the cages our hearts heavy knowing dogs that don't get picked are likely put to sleep.

In each cage frightened dogs greeted us. Their soulful eyes begging us closer to get the merest touch of human contact. They look at us, legs trembling. Some climb the metal screens their noses and tongues pushing through the small gaps.

There were no Labrador pups and the staff reminded us it was not a shop where you picked a breed you wanted. It was a rescue centre, and it was our job to try and save one dog be it a known breed or a Heinz 57, mongrel.

We went into each cage many of the dogs suspicious and backing off frightened of this intrusion. There was a right mix, and many of the dogs came toward us, tentatively. Once we kneeled down to pet them, it was like a rush with them all trying to climb all over us licking us to death.

The staff look after the animals so well and do their best not to get attached. One staff member told us she wanted to make sure each dog had fun in the park, walked and hugged each night.

A small ball of fur walked towards us out of the melee, it was the size of a hedgehog. It sat in front of us and licked our hands his blue eyes staring and a nervous tail wag. Like all dog owners we knew immediately he was the one. Black, with a white flash across his chest he sat proudly looking at us.

'He's the one, I said, and the staff member picked him up. 'You are a little cutie' she said cuddling into him.

Our dog was chipped and given injections while we filled out the relevant paperwork. We were now the proud owners of a Border Collie, not a Labrador and we couldn't be happier. We donated to the centre, and the staff came out waving us off or more likely, our little bundle.

We headed back to our home in Argyll discussing names all the way. It's such a hard thing to do because it has to suit the dog and he has to live with it for life. The last thing a dog wants is a name like Snookums, especially when playing next to an Alsatian in the park called Rex. ;0)

We tried looking for names online and wanted it to have a quality sound. Brenda was designing on her Apple computer that evening when she came through to me. 'I've got his name' she said, looking pleased with herself. I'd already heard 250 names, so I was sure it was just another one of the long list.

'Macintosh' she said, We can call him Mac for short. At that point, out little bundle sat up and walked towards her. 'Macintosh it is then.' I said.

To be continued. Everyone loves Mac. Mac digs a hole through the middle of our Champagne coloured three-piece-suite. Mac, and Us go Dog Training.

21

HOW TIMES CHANGE

A Poem from 1968 to 1977

Woodstock Festival, long flowing hair
Psychedelic times, free love was in the air
Flower power, music, mind-freeing drugs
Baez sang sweetly while Shankar played his stuff

Buddhism and mystics burn patchouli incense
Freedom from society, it was all less intense

Smoking and peace signs, and 'keep off the grass'
Daisy chains and dancing, get naked, shake ass

Aldrin and Armstrong had the best views in town
As the world looked up, they were looking down
John Lennon and Yoko were tucked up in bed
Whilst his friend Mr Harrison tried to help Bangladesh

The lights were all out, the power shut down
A three day week, no strength in our pound
The 'troubles' were growing, we feared the IRA
It all went wrong one bloody Sunday

Vietnam was burning, from blunder burst attacks
Agent Orange and Napalm there was no holding back
War fuelled Americans took their fight to Saigon
Nixon was caught, apologies, he's gone

Mr Dali bent paintings and played with our minds
Whilst Uri bent spoons he played to the blind
'the Big Yin' had Parkinson rolling in stitches
The Tartan Army stole goalposts from Wembley's pitches

Sideburns, thick glasses, true crimes and passion
Westwood and McLaren sold SEX and weird fashion
Political correctness didn't seem as unhealthy
Love thy neighbour and Garnett were both on the telly

The music was changing it was loud and quite rough
Razor blades and chains and spitting and stuff
Spiked hair, Mohicans, studs through their tongues
Johnny Rotten and Sid Vicious swore on BBC1

It came to a peak, new wave versus rock

They said a music revolution, but it was mostly all talk
Then the world's heart stopped beating 'the King, Elvis
had died!'
The most handsome of men, a generation cried

22

THE MAN IN THE MOON

There was an old man from Dunoon
Who made a rocket out of balloons
He twisted and twanged
then his rocket went bang
And now he resides on the moon

23

ROCKET MAN MEETS TWEETER TRUMP

Donald Trump has Scottish blood in his veins
He's thrifty in business, many think he's insane
He likes to get everyone to do things his way
Whether trade wars or high walls, he wants others to pay

He fights for his people, there's naught wrong with that
I wonder if we'd gain from having our own autocrat
He's fixing the economy, world leaders, handshakes
Increasing employment, so his people have a stake

Collusion with Russia, rogue meetings, fake advertising

Democrats have never done this, so they say, that's
surprising
All elections have been tainted, since the first ballot box
And it won't ever change, Russians, Chinese or despots

Stormy was paid, plus a bonus for not talking
150Ks not enough, to the media she went hawking
Can the Donald claim a refund, for his expensive spanking
After all where's his extras and a note just to thank him

The storm's followed him home now Melania's not talking
She'd leave if she could, but we won't see her walking
Her composure is stoic, glassy stare and no tears
She prays that he falters, she can't take four more years

The media he's tackled like no one else dare
His weapon is Twitter, fifty-two million share
Fake news he shouts, rejecting the Whitehouse press corp
He won't join them for dinner, he's no journalists whore

When it comes to women, Donald, gets it all wrong
His vile locker-room talk should have seen him long gone
Misogynist and predatory, grabbing women by their
genitals
This alpha male stance is by no way acceptable

The Paris agreement, Donald thinks it's a ruse
No emissions or over-heating, he hasn't a clue
Yet his country has lived through the most violent storms
With Katrina and Irma, people's lives ripped and torn

With weapons and guns, he's certainly confused
He talks of London where knives have stabbed quite a few
Yet his own students slaughtered, by automatic guns

And the NRAs solution, give everyone one

The G7 leadership try to curb this man's wants
A businessman against politicians they don't stand a
chance
He's survived dog eat dog deals for most of his life
These mild-mannered politicians are frankly too nice

The two funniest haircuts have arrived in Singapore
Rocketman and tweeter Trump will settle old scores
We might forgive This President for his unorthodox ways
If he brings peace to Korea, and get people set free

I'm still undecided if he's good or he stinks
His actions disruptive but he makes us all think
History will tell when he's scrutinised through the lens
Did he achieve his ambition, to make "America Great
Again'

24

MAC GOES TO SCHOOL - PART 2

LAST EPISODE I GAVE AN INTRODUCTION TO OUR BORDER COLLIE, MacIntosh. Well, every dog has to have a Sunday name, during the week he was Mac.

So a border collie we had, and he was the cutest little ball of fluff ever - butter wouldn't melt, if you get my meaning.

We lived in Innellan, near Dunoon and across from our house was a small forest which was the ideal play area for him. Each morning one of us would take him for a runaround, and he loved it. He loved nothing better than to disappear into the undergrowth for a good old snuffle. He wasn't good at returning and hadn't learnt that shouting his name out loud meant he was to come back to us. We used to search for ages. More often than not he'd appear from under the carpet of wild garlic that spread across the forest floor.

Mac was getting bigger and wouldn't walk or do what was expected from him when he was on the lead. He preferred to fight and shake his head to be free from the long extending line of string. Our neighbour suggested we take him to the old hall in Dunoon for Dog Training classes.

Dog Training Classes - First Night

What can I say except we weren't prepared. Until that night Mac hadn't met many dogs and cowered at the howling and barking as we entered.

A woman with a commanding voice instructed me to put him on the floor to get used to the other dogs. I knew this was a bad idea from the start. I could see how nervous he was with the number of dogs crowded around him. From Yorkshire terriers to Alsatians they were all in full sniff mode.

His poor wee legs were shaking uncontrollably, I picked him up to comfort him.

'Leave him - put him down' the instructor shouted, man her voice was loud. She gave me the beady eye.

Mac continued shaking and then the fear took over in the way that nervous dogs do - he did a number two on the floor. One of the helpers handed me a roll of kitchen towel and told me to wipe it up. I wasn't really good at that as I was struggling enough at home with nappies - I handed the roll to Brenda who gave it straight back to me. It was your idea to come here - she mouthed.

Mac had enough. He ran, with his lead trailing behind him straight under the benches that made the perimeter of the hall.

He got stuck behind the old fashioned heating pipes trying to escape the dogs who were in hot pursuit of him. By the time I got to him, he was in a sorry state covered in years of church hall fluff. I blew the dust from him like you'd do with a dandelion.

Inspection

The woman in charge called out in that voice again.

'Can all dog owners come to the centre of the floor with their dogs on their leads.'

Dogs were clipped on and taken to the centre of the room. Our instructor walked the line inspecting us. Any dog that jumped up was shown the palm of her hand and pushed back firmly. She took my extending lead and replaced it with a green canvas strap.

'Why are you all here?' she shouted.

'To get our dogs trained.' we managed to reply in an awkward unison which dwindled away to an incomprehensible murmur.

'Wrong, she said. Try again. Why are you all here?'

No one answered. Eyes looking at each other. I felt like I was in Primary One again

'We're not here to train the dogs, she pointed at us, we're here to train you. When a dog misbehaves, it's not the dog's fault, you are the problem.'

I stood terrified, my days of standing outside the headmaster's office were filling my head. I was sure this woman could read my thoughts.

Heel

'We'd only been here ten minutes and I wanted to go home.'

I followed her instructions walking round in circles and pulling the lead every time Mac strayed.

'Two sharp pulls with the command 'heel'. she shouted.

Every time she spoke she doubled up with a hand signal. The dogs definitely understood the signals better than English. If I were anywhere else, I would've cracked a joke and told her dogs only speak Doglish, but I was too scared of her.

Tea Break

Thankfully, the interval arrived. We sat down for tea and biscuits and a few of the dogs were drooling waiting for a tidbit. The woman next to me gave me a nudge.

'Aww, look at his wee face, he's a real smasher.' She threw a piece of biscuit towards Mac and just as I was about to warn her a voice erupted from across the hall.

'Don't ever feed a dog human food.'

The woman crumbled. I felt bad for her as she had given the treat to our dog. We watched as she got a proper dressing down which was a wee bit harsh for a first night. Not the best approach for long-term customer loyalty.

Our trainer continued, 'You'll learn when it comes to dogs, I'm always right.' she said.

And so, tea over, Tunnock's teacake taken care of, we started the second half of the night's meeting.

I decided I'd had enough walking up and down and so I sat on the benches. It was Brenda's turn to control Mac and seeing as she thought I was doing it all wrong I was pleased to pass the mantle to her. I watched as she walked around the hall to the sound of the heel command.

The Tunnel

Two assistants lifted a bright red circle from a bag. One brought out a long tunnel you know the kind kids get at an adventure park. The other had a cane with two cones.

Our instructor informed us of the next lesson.

'You have to get your dog to jump over the stick and then run through the tunnel. Once you put your dog into the entrance leave them, go to the other end of the tunnel and call your dog's name. Is that clear?'

Lots of mumbling again from the dog owners.

The instructor took her dog Rusty which leapt over the stick and ran through the tunnel without effort.

'Good boy, she said clapping him. She took a dog treat from her pocket and gave it to the well-trained springer spaniel.

Like the other newbies, I wasn't impressed. I'm sure we were all thinking her dog does this every week. If she's done it with Mac I might have been impressed.

The first three dog owners managed to get their dogs through the tunnel after a lot of prompting and dragging.

'Practice is all it takes.' our trainer shouted.

I was trying to think at what point would I ever take my dog and throw him into a tunnel. I started to think about how stupid it was when she called out Mac's name. Oh, that's another thing - at dog training owners become insignificant. They lose their identity. Everything is referred to around your dog's name. I was no longer Grahame - Big Chief of the Anderson's - no, now I was Mac's dad and Brenda was Mac's mum.

I watched as Brenda took Mac to the stick - 'Jump' she said, Mac sat down and sniffed at the stick.

'Jump... jump...jump.'

With each command Brenda lifted his lead higher and higher his neck stretching until his paws left the floor. She raised him a little higher and swung him over the cane.

'Good Boy' she said. The trainer shook her head.

Next, Brenda ran Mac across the hall over to the entrance of the tunnel and unclipped his lead.

'Go on, she said. Run through.'

Mac looked into the tunnel and didn't move. I could tell he was freaked out. Brenda pushed his bottom and then threw him into the entrance a couple of feet, but he turned and ran back.

This was fun, I was savouring every moment. I knew Mac wouldn't go through.

'If a dog doesn't go through the tunnel, the owner must show them how. 'Can Mac's mum please get down and crawl through the tunnel.'

Brenda's eyes met mine - she was doing that silent thing only a woman can do, instructing me to go over and bale her out. It was like the scene from Bonnie and Clyde. She stared at me, and I stared back and then at my nails ignoring her not wanting to get involved.

'Please, get down and crawl through the tunnel.'

Brenda got down on all fours - not a good thing to do in skin-tight jeans. Her bum looked wider than Chicago. I wasn't convinced the nylon tunnel would survive this much of a beating as she made her way through. (You know the way an elephant's bum really moves from side to side when it walks - well it was nothing like that, wahaha!)

Brenda bravely crawled through dragging Mac behind her. Our instructor telling Brenda what to do but she couldn't hear her for us laughing.

Brenda emerged from the far end of the tunnel, flustered.

'Give me some wipes,' she said - some dog has peed inside the tunnel - look at my knees.'

Sure enough two large dark patches on her jeans.

'Dog training you said. It'll be a laugh. You can take him yourself next week.' she said.

It was a quiet journey home in the car. Smelled funny.

The next day we saw the funny side of it.

25

THE STAG DO

YE KNOW THERE'S NO MANY THINGS THAT ANNOY ME BUT SEE going to Prestwick Airport, that really cheeses me aff. So here ah um, travelling wi' the boys tae the airport for the early flight tae Barcelona. Ah don't even want to go there. I couldnae think of anywhere worse in the world. Aw them foreigners and the food will no be tae ma liking.

Anyway, we're going on a stag do. But Prestwick! How could it no be Glesga? It's just doon the street fur god sake! It's wan o those stupid things that annoys me. Why do we need Prestwick Airport?

How come it tries to kid on it's part of Glesga when it's naewhere near it? Ah'm a Paisley boy and ah expect tae jump on a bus that takes two minutes tae the 'real airport'. But naw, instead ah've got tae cadge a lift doon the coast tae catch ma plane.

An' that's another thing that really pisses me aff. When you arrive at Prestwick the first thing ye see is their slogan emblazoned across the ootside of the building. 'Pure Dead Brilliant.'

Whit idiot thought that wan up. People fae aw o'er the world don't want tae interpret the word deid - it's a local joke. It shouldnae be oan an international building. Ah gist don't get it. Whit idiot in charge thought that wis acceptable.

Anyway, as always, because of the crazy five o'clock time we had tae leave hame, in the freezin' cold. I'm still wonderin' how ah managed tae get out ma bed at this god awful time. This is definitely no ma normal bag but sometimes ye hiv tae dae whit ye hiv tae dae!

Ah watch the big screens while the rest o' the lads...well let's just say, they think it's time tae get the party rollin'. Who ever thought a pint o' freezin' cold lager, or Guinness, or worse still, for them wi' a discerning pallet, 'bottled craft beers' wis whit wis needed first thing in the morning. Ah cannae go that, ah've no even lined my stomach yet.

So that ah'm no a moanin' old sod, ah decide to avoid the drinking activities and keep ma eye oan the flight screens. Big Geordie, who's a bloody eejit by the way, is trying to send me a sign, holding an invisible gless an kidding on he's drinking it. Ah'm avoiding eye contact wi' them aw, as it's better if I look as if I'm naw wae them.

It's naw just the Prestwick Airport thing that annoys me, it's the whole 'modern stag' going abroad stupidity. How come we cannae jist huv a stag do in the local boozer like the old days? Who thought taking fifteen grown men, wan dressed as a rabbit, away fur four days tae Barcelona, wi' aw that expense wis a good idea? Ah've hid to borrow money for this nonsense.

Anyhoo, ah don't know why ah'm moanin', cos ah've no say in it anyway. Ma nephew wanted it. And as ma brother's deid, not pure deid, jist deid, ah've got tae let ma nephew huv his party. Well so ma wife says.

'They need a responsible adult' she shouted at me. Ah thought that wis the biggest joke oh them aw, cos ah've never been responsible in ma life. Ah cannae even make my ain tea, and here I am in charge of fifteen doughnuts, who if you took aw their brains oot and joined them together yi' might jistaboot make wan good wan. Well maybe naw!

Ah'm searching the flight screens again hoping they gie us a gate number quick so's ah can stop them drinking any more. I'm noo acting like I'm no way them and to be honest I wish I wisnae. The passengers are looking nervous, families and business people, looking nonchalant on the outside but inside they are praying. Ah see the fear on their faces. You know that look, the wan that screams 'Ah better no be sitting next to them.' Well funny enough that's how I feel aboot travelling wi' ma lot tae. Actually I jist want tae go back up the road tae Paisley.

The boys are noo stoatin' an' starting to swear and using the c word, naw a good sign. Jeez ah've seen it a thousand times. They're aw telling each other tae knock the drink back faster. Oor groom, Thumper, has his heid hinging aff and looks peely-wally. By ma estimates he's aboot five minutes fae throwing up. West of Scotland drinking - who needs it?

The lads are too loud fir comfort and getting right oot of order. They're singing Bright Eyes to our rabbit who's heid is back on. They're lining up more booze as if the barman's aboot tae call time. 'Here Andy get wan doon ye.' wan o' them shouts tae me.

Ah turn and head to WH Smith acting as if ah didnae here him. Ah need tae get a Daily Record and some sports mixtures. I need them fur ma ears when takin' aff and landin'.

When you think about it whit is that pish we all live wi'? Get wan doon ye. Where did this come fae? An it disnae even matter whit drink it is - as long as it's alcohol and can knock ye dizzy. Ah don't get it.

I looked over tae the door and wis hoping ma eyes were deceiving me. The normal people were shifting awkwardly in their seats again at the approaching sight. Twelve Glesga girls dressed in Pink Cowboy outfits on a hen do singing 'We just blew in from the windy city'. Jeez is ma life no bad enough. Ah hope 'am no sittin' next to them.

The barman must be eighteen and not very good at his job. He wid ne'er get a job in a Paisley pub as he cannae cope wi' the flurry of new orders. Spritzer, Gins, Bacardi and cokes, the orders are flying at him. That's another thing that annoys me, the speed them lassies can knock back the drink, some o' them are drinking faster than my squad.

An look at their clothes, ah'm seeing too much skin fur ma liking. If it's no bellies on display it's skirts that are hardly longer than their pants. They couldnae bend doon tae pick up a ten-pence wi oot lookin' as if they were working in a Soho nightclub.

I look at the rest of the cavalry. Some of them wummin' look as if they've been squeezed into them pink cowboy suits rather than buying the right size. If they untied the laces at the front it would be like a bouncy castle self-inflating. Maybe it's jist me and I don't get the fashion. Maybe they want it all hinging oot the front if they're trying to get a lumber. Where's their modesty?

It's the tattoos defacing their bodies that gets me. Whit's that aw aboot? Between this lot they've got more tattoos than a Hells Angel Chapter. You can see them creeping up their backs, just above their bum cracks when they bend over, it's no a pretty sight.

That's another thing, how come every second person noo, has to have a tattoo? I'm not against them if they were done discreetly. But seriously, we've got great big things across thighs, full arm sleeves, scenes across their backs, not to mention the trend of being on the neck and face. An' half of them tattoos don't look that pretty. Whit will these wummin' look like at seventy, lying in a hospital bed covered in that shit. 'It's art' they say. Art my arse, if you want art go and buy yersel' a painting.

Oh oh! one o' the airline wummin' is rounding up my team. Ah can tell she's airline because she has a flying uniform on. She's talking to the lads and they're all shaking their heads. She has two polis standing next tae her as she delivers the bad news tae ma party.

'Due to excessive alcohol intake you are not allowed to fly today'. My question is, why are they bloody selling alcohol at five in the morning. Open yer bar at eleven in the morning like everyone else. Ah go over tae see them. It wis aw ma nephews fault for throwing up, through his rabbit outfits mesh mouth, jist as he was picking up his lasagne in the self-service queue. That wis wan step too far fir the airline.

'Whit's happening?' I asked him, still dressed in his rabbit onesy, yellow stains around the mouth and smelling bad.'

'That cow told us we're no getting oan the plane!

'Whit, are ye sure?'

'Aye. An' the next plane tae Barcelona isnae fir three days an the boys ah've aw got jobs tae go tae on Monday. So we've decided we're aw going back tae Paisley and sit in the pub there, try get a lock-in. Better go and collect your case Uncle Andy, they're separating oors oot from the rest o' the plane's.'

'Ah'm sorry son. Ah'm off tae Barcelona, ah've no been drinking and ah borrowed money for this gig, so ah'm still going.'

'But you'll miss ma stag do.'

'Ah will son, but ah don't want tae miss ma trip. Ah've been really looking forward tae Barcelona. I couldnae think of a better place ah want tae be, the culture and the exciting food an aw that.'

The rabbit turned and walked away his fluffy tail hanging off.

His outfit wasn't zipped properly at the back and he was showing off his fake Calvin Klein underwear.

The Calamity Janes struck up another song. 'Dancing Queen.'

I certainly don't remember Doris Day singing that in the film.

'Oh God, ah hope ah'm no sitting next tae them.'

26

A RIGHT ROYAL DO

I see down in London there's a right Royal do
and it's been watched by millions, right about noo
It's taking place at the venue, an historic old castle
The two main characters, Oor Harry and Ms Markle

There's horses, wi' carriages displaying oor Meghan
We've cleared streets of the homeless, well we can't show
them beggin'
The media coverage has been all inter-racial
Do we have to mention this about the love of two people?

I saw the food and cakes, the sprinkles and jelly
It's so bloody tempting on our Hi-def telly
The streets lined with flags and bunting' and stuff
Security's high, there can never be enough

The Prince of Wales is giving Meghan away
As her poor dad's sick, his heart's given way
Harry watches Meghan as she comes down the aisle,
his dreams come true as he watches her smile

And so they come out in all their splendour
The bride in her dress, looking ever so slender
Harry looks good, scrubbed up in his best
But the bride is the focus, in her designer dress

The band strikes up, the cavalry in display
As they lead the couple, all waving away
They head to the party, for a drink and a dance
The beginning of their journey, one beautiful romance

There's talk of the rings, the bride's has more sparkle
Harry's is plain, he can't outshine Ms Markle
They stare at each other, their eyes say the lot
On the day that they married and tied that old knot

As the streets start clearing, only rubbish left behind
The crowds head home, marching slowly in time
The people feel closer, texts of love they've been sending
To their partners and loved ones about this fairytale
ending

© Grahame Anderson Storyteller - May 19th 2018

27

GHOST STORY

NIGEL SCREAMED. HIS MOTHER RUSHED TO HIS ROOM. HE WAS shaking and pointing at the mirror. 'A ghost!'

She looked and saw an old man with part of his head sliced off laughing while sharpening a knife covered in blood. She followed the reflection. Her husband dressed for Halloween smirked!

28

NEIGHBOURS, TRA-LA-LA-LA-LA

I'm not your normal touchy-feely guy
My head's full of strategies and visions to fly
I'm not good with kids unless they're my own
If anything, however, it's my neighbours I disown

It's not that they're wrong or even I'm right
I don't discuss sheds or security lights
The weather, dog fouling or the latest wind chimes
I only want to live here and just do my time

It doesn't sound friendly I humbly confess
But I couldn't care less about number fifteen's new dress
or washing the car, manicuring the lawn
listening to this, well, I just start to yawn

I'm fine with hello, how are you today?
As I walk to my car for my quick getaway
You can borrow my ladder, hedge trimmers, or brush
Just don't get me involved when discussing some fuss

Who knows who? Who's doing what?
No 5 left her man, I couldn't give a jot
The dog at 28 ate poison from the shed
An expensive mishap and a night at the vets

The redhead with tattoos is having an affair
With her stilettos, split skirts, she really does dare
In a car, in the dark, hot breath, steamed windows
Her husband, the minister, shouldn't have married a
bimbo

Let's have a Facebook group for the neighbours to talk
Pictures and friends and 'Do you know who said what!'
No 7 is friends with my half brother's cousin
That's the level of drivel I find no point discussing

From what you have read there may be the suggestion
That I don't like anyone, well that's just your impression
My thoughts are clear, I'm sure they're nice neighbours
But I prefer if they ignore me - and do me that favour. ;0)

Please note - no neighbours were hurt in the making of
this poem ;0) wahaha!

29

COUNTRY FAIR - BLACKBIRD BY THE BEATLES REWRITTEN

THE FOLLOWING WRITING WAS AN EXERCISE AT MY WRITERS' CLUB. We had to pick a Beatles song and change the words but make it feel like the music was written for our words. I chose the track Blackbird and changed the lyrics to Country Fair. I feel the lyrics suit the music - so very pleased with this.

We're all going to the country fair
Where people dance and wear flowers through their hair
Once a year

We stand waiting patiently, for the circus to appear

We're all going to the country fair
where the band keep playing and the guests all eat their
share
We're all full
Now we raise our glasses for another successful year

Country fair, country fair
We can't wait till you come again next year

We're all going to the country fair
Where lovers kiss and kids play truth or dare
Last slow da -nce
now we wave goodbye as the field's left scorched and bare
now we wave goodbye as the field's left scorched and bare
now we wave goodbye as the field's left scorched and bare

30

ASSASSIN'S PRAYER

...Bless me father for I have sinned

Chorus
Our Father who art in heaven
Bless my protectors one through seven

Give my family their daily bread
Kill my enemies, kill them dead

Verse 1
Kiss my robes, sign the cross
Bless my messengers of the cloth
Love thy neighbour turn the cheek
Hunt them down kill the meek

Oh father dear father please forgive me
As I walk this path I plea for redemption
I know the angels have walked beside me
But Christ or Satan who is it that guides me?

My knuckles bleed with Love and Hate
The sword of truth at Heaven's Gate
My spirits gone who's right who's wrong
Get behind me it's far too long

I move in darkness through the night
Find my prey and deliver death or fright
Point the gun pull hard on the trigger
Her legs collapse as she hears me snigger

Break the bread drink the wine
Kiss the ring. I'm feeling fine
I'll walk on the Lord's side I'm sure he knows
as I help him wipe out this scum that grows

Chorus

It's the drugs, the rackets, the women and girls
controlled by this element all slick backed and chilled
Greasy bastards destroy communities from within

Risking their families perpetuating this shit

I promise you father to cleanse this world
of this filth they've forced upon our catholic girls
Their pimps I'll destroy they bring me no fear
I'm protected by the madonna and the strength of her
    tears

31
A DOLL FOR CHRISTMAS

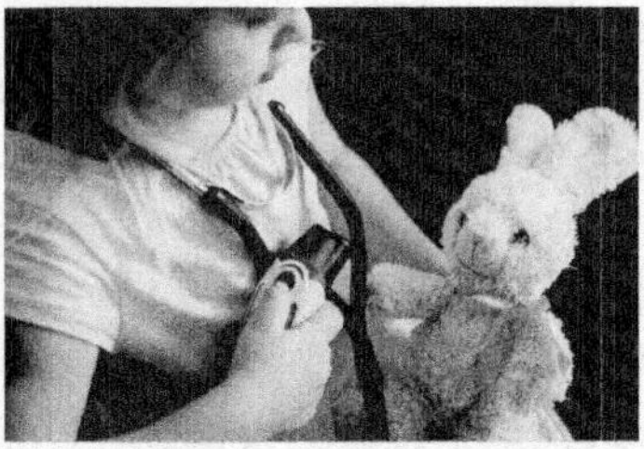

GORDON DROVE SLOWLY THROUGH THE THICK FOG. HE STRUGGLED to see the road ahead and wiped furiously with his cloth over the ever misting windscreen. Visibility was less than twenty feet. He groaned as the weather became worse, with heavy snow falling.

'Bloody hell! Snow is the last thing I need, I can't remember ever seeing snow and fog at the same time'.

His lights battled to pierce through the thick blanket of fog, his wipers working overtime at double speed.

He looked at his wife Mary, who sat quietly, not wanting to interrupt or add to his stress. One hand held onto the handle above the door while her other was twisting her coat belt as the tension became too much for her.

'I think you should stop. We can leave the car, she said. This is too dangerous.'

Her husband looked at her. 'Oh really, and where do you suggest I leave it? Just abandon it here in the middle of nowhere. I want to get home as soon as we can and get back to the kids.'

Mary bit her lip while remaining silent. If she mentioned stopping once more he would blow a gasket.

Visibility was down to a few feet. The wipers could barely clear the window quickly enough.

He glanced across at her. 'Stop fretting. Five minutes and we'll be home.'

'Can we park and walk the final few hundred yards. The car is sliding at every turn,' Mary said.

'It's only three more streets for God's sake. Stop panicking you're not helping,' he shouted.

They both screamed as something thumped against the windscreen leaving a pattern of mosaic glass as the windscreen shattered. Blood ran down the window before being smeared across the screen by the wipers. They both froze!

Gordon threw the car door open and stepped out into the blizzard his body shocked at the change in temperature. On the silent snow covered street his elderly neighbour Alfie lay still a halo of blood spreading slowly from his head. There was no movement. Gordon looked at a Christmas present lying beside his neighbour its wrapping ripped open. A doll stared back out at him. Written on the tag , To the best Granddaughter Ever, Love Grandad.

32

HOW TO KILL YOUR MOTHER

ASHFIELD, AN OLD VICTORIAN HOUSE, SITS AT THE END OF A LONG driveway. Painted white and finished with a burgundy colour on the doors, windows, and eaves, it was obvious, even to an untrained eye, this house had fallen on hard times by the state of disrepair.

Inside, a mother lived with her adult son, Stephen. Aged forty two, he works from a desk in the corner of his bedroom, his daily routine now for many years. Suffering from writers' block today has not been a good day. Staring at his typewriter dismayed at what he has written, he pulls the sheet of paper from the rollers, scrunching it up he throws it over his shoulder towards a waste basket if it could be found under the clothes and assorted items that covered the floor. Frustrated, he paced the floor, his breathing heavy.

Round the room he walked in a pattern he'd done many times. He heard a noise and looked outside. The wind had whipped up and the trees bordering his garden were swaying back and forth robustly. The noise was deafening and his window frame rattled. A few howls from the wind that squeezed through the gaps into his room, forcing a high-pitched whistling noise like an out-of-control kettle. He picked up a t-shirt and stuffed it into the space the wind still whistling as it forced its way into the house. Leaves blew off the trees and disappeared into the distance.

His mother, carrying a large basket of washing struggling against the fierce wind as she headed towards the washing line. Stephen watched in disbelief as she tried to hold on to a shirt which was being ripped out of her hands. He watched her struggle. She looked up and saw him standing at the window and shouted for him to come down and help. He made a sign to mimic he couldn't hear her and walked away from the window. He sat down and typed a few lines.

An hour later his mother called him to come down for his lunch. They sat at the kitchen table, eating their soup, mostly in silence.

'Are you going to sit up there all day doing nothing?' she asked.

'I'm not doing nothing as you call it. I'm writing! How many times do I have to tell you,' he said?

There was an uncomfortable silence.

'I was thinking it's time you earned a living, you know, bring in some money. We could do with some extra. It's getting harder to keep the house and live on what I bring in.'

Stephen looked at her. He placed his spoon on the table, stood up and headed back to his room.

She shook her head. What was she to do with him? Forty-two

years old, living at home, no friends, no girlfriend and no motivation, except writing. From what she had read of his work, some of it was good, however, after eight years of working solid she had only ever seen excerpts of stories that were never completed. It was time to change this. She called an old friend, Ian, who owned a factory and asked if he could give Stephen a job. The time, she thought, had arrived.

Stephen picked a book from his bookshelf 'Be a Creative Writer'. He flicked through the pages. It was the same formula he had read in so many books about writing. Every story had to have a similar set of parameters: protagonist, antagonist, plot, location, characters, victim and lots of conflict. He knew this stuff inside out. A simple recipe on writing. There was nothing difficult about it, except the one missing ingredient that most of the book rarely mentioned. The same thing all 'How to Write' books missed in their formula for a successful story - IMAGINATION.

Stephen knew this was the missing ingredient. It was the one true piece of value in every story that couldn't be taught as part of a formula. No imagination, no original story.

He thought about writing. Anyone can pick a place, name a detective, place a victim in a location and decide on their fate. A gunshot wound to the head, or kidnapped, maybe thrown from a moving vehicle, the lists were endless. These parts were easy.

Original imagination however, the unique skill necessary for every writer to weave a repeatable set of features, successfully into a scene that comes alive. He started to type again.

Downstairs, the front door slammed.

He got up from his chair and looked out. Not again. How many laundry washes can one person do in a day? The most he'd counted her doing was six. That was her record. He watched her struggle against the wind. She was checking the first wash to see how dry it was. She removed some clothes off the line and placed them into her basket and hung the wet clothes out. She looked up to see Stephen at the window again. She waved for him to come down and carry her filled basket back into the house. He stepped back once more. She shouted out 'lazy good for nothing'.

She chased her empty peg bag down the garden where it clung to a hedge. Struggling for breath she walked back, peg bag grasped firmly in hand.

Stephen watched her every move. She would make a good victim, he thought. He tried a few scenarios in his head. An elderly woman living alone in a large house. Someone comes walking up the path and strangles her with her washing line, even better they could put that pillowcase over her head, tie her hands and hit her with the shovel leaning against the wall. What would be their motive? He mused. An unbalanced neighbour, sick of her Leylandii hedges growing twenty-five feet high blocking out the light to their garden - that could work, he thought. Where would they hide her body? No point in the garden, too easy for the police. Better to move it from the scene of the crime and dispose of it in a forest at least thirty miles away. Stephen mulled over his story. He put a new sheet of A4 into his typewriter. He typed his title and sat back to look at it. He grinned and read it out loud 'HOW TO KILL YOUR MOTHER' by Stephen.

He was in a dream state for over two hours imagining a host of different scenarios when his mother shouted for him to come down for his 'tea'.

'It's called dinner mum, not tea. Tea means something else completely.'

His mum placed a plate of mince and potatoes in front of him.

'Here's your tea, Mr Wordsworth. If you want to eat 'dinner' and don't recognise this as your 'tea' then don't eat it.'

She dished out a plate for herself. They both ate quietly. The only sound was the ticking of the large grandfather clock that sat in the hallway. His mum was looking at him strangely. He could tell she was getting ready to say something. She shifted from side to side uneasily and put her knife and fork down on her plate. He thought of escaping to his room. She cleared her throat.

'We need to talk,' she said.

'Do we?'

'Yes, we do. I think it's time you started to pull yourself together, ' she said. 'You've been working on your writing for eight years now. After that length of time, I would expect to see something completed from that level of effort. But when I assess it you haven't produced one finished story that you've shown me. You don't talk to other writers or go to classes to discuss how they approach writing, so how can you possibly develop and learn?

'Save me the big speech mum. I can't handle this.'

She ignored his interruption and continued.

'My thoughts are this. You should give up writing as a full-time career, get a job at the factory and write as a hobby in the evenings.'

'I'm not working at the factory. I'm a writer.'

'You are not a writer. You have nothing to show for that statement except a cupboard full of unfinished stories and hard as it is for me to say this, I think it's time you faced the truth about your career choice as a so-called writer. Who will ever read your unfinished story parts that hide, tucked away in your cupboard?'

'Van Gogh only sold one painting in his lifetime and that was to his brother Theo. Now the art world is clambering for his paintings worldwide.'

'Yes, but he actually finished his paintings. Unlike Van Gogh, we can't afford to live here anymore with just my salary. You're not even claiming support. I'm not prepared to discuss this any further. Tomorrow morning, shave and shower. I've organised an interview for you.'

Stephen shook his head.

'I'm not looking for a job. I don't do manual labour.'

'Correction, you don't do any labour.'

'I will not work in that factory.'

'Why not? It's full of people. People with character. People who are potentially the basis of new stories every day. Don't you get it. These are the things you need to experience, to see and observe. This is where you find all the little hidden gems, the catalysts to write stories from. If you don't engage with the world, you will never have nothing to write about. Think of all the strange quirks and oddities and how strange the other workers will be. Don't see this job as work, see it as a fertile feeding ground for your writing material. Your wage will only be a bonus.'

Stephen finished 'his tea' and went back to his room. He sat in front of his typewriter thinking about what his mother had said and fell asleep. Next morning his alarm clock was ringing in the background. He didn't feel good. He had a sore neck and stiff back from sitting upright all night in his chair. He struggled to his feet and headed downstairs for breakfast.

'Why aren't you shaved and dressed for your interview?' his mother asked.

'I told you yesterday, I will not go to work'

'You better move fast, she said, ignoring his last comment. 'One of Ian's men will pick you up in twenty minutes.' Stephen looked at her.

'If you want to go to work, you go. I've got a full day of writing ahead of me.'

His mother slammed her hand on the table hard making him jump. She picked up a knife quickly and thrust it towards his face. He immediately drew back. She leaned in close, almost nose to nose with him and through gritted teeth gave him a very terse warning.

'Get yourself up those stairs and get ready for work, right now!'

Stephen got up from the table. He had never seen his mother

this mad. He went up to his room. He paced in circles for five minutes, trying to clear his head. The doorbell rang. He could hear the conversation travelling up the stairwell. His mother's shouted up,

'Stephen, are you ready? Ian's driver is here for you.' Stephen opened his bedroom door.

'Sorry mum, didn't I say this morning I wasn't feeling well. Maybe next week.'

'Okay. I'll tell the driver.'

Stephen stood at the top of the stairs. He heard his mum apologise profusely. The car drove off. His mother screamed and smashed a pile of plates. Two minutes later, the front door slammed as she left for work. Stephen smiled and sat at his typewriter. He looked at his sheet of paper again, HOW TO KILL YOUR MOTHER, he started to write. He thought he now had the recipe for a good story. He started to type. Suddenly it all began to flow. A story was forming in his head. He put it down on paper as fast as he could. For the first time in eight years of writing he had worked it out. All those bits and pieces and how to join them together. It was the imagination part he just had to set free. All the other parts were just a formula. Imagination was everything. It's all about delivering surprise to the reader when they least expect it.

Suddenly he's surprised by his mother walking into his bedroom, shouting at him. She is furious. Didn't she leave for work an hour ago? He thought.

'How dare you embarrass me this morning? You need to take responsibility for yourself and join the real world. Sitting here in a fantasy land, day-dreaming. I want you out working or out of this house. Stephen stood up. He tried to calm her down.

"Take it easy mum, I'll get some money. I promise. Maybe my next story will be a big hit. '

'Don't be so bloody stupid.' she said. 'How can you sell

anything if you never finish a story? It's time to admit that you are utterly useless at writing.'

Stephen saw red. A mist came down over his eyes. How could his mother talk to him like this? He walked away from her but she grabbed his shoulder.

'I want you out working' she screamed in his face.

Stephen picked up his typewriter and hit her on the side of the head. She hit the floor in one fluid movement. There was no struggle, no twitching, no convulsing, she was out cold. Stephen checked her pulse. Nothing. She wasn't out cold; she was dead. He panicked. He grabbed her by the ankles and dragged her down the stairs feet first. Her head bumping hard off every step, no doubt leaving a trail of evidence. He lay her body on the kitchen floor and picked up the broken plates she had smashed earlier. He cut his hand with a sliver of plate and now he had blood dripping everywhere. He found a large decorators polythene sheet and wrapped her body in it. He took a roll of tape and wrapped her tightly. Her face was looking at him. He placed tape over the area where her eyes were staring at him. He carried her body out to her car and opened the boot. It was full of junk. He emptied the boot and placed her body in the car. It surprised him how light she was only because every time he had written about a body being moved he had always said how heavy a dead weight was. Now he knew for his next book he could state that the body was light. He locked his mother's body in the boot. He would dispose of it tonight. He ran upstairs and cleaned the typewriter. He typed up some notes. Suddenly he had all the answers. He put it all down as fast as he could type. He had the characters, the victim, the plot, the scene, the murder and the body disposal. It had all come together. His fingers hammered the keys joyously putting the story together. He punched the air a few times shouting Yes! For the very first time since he called himself a writer he typed the two most incredible meaningful words in the English language 'THE END' on the last page of his manuscript.

He had successfully finished his first story. Stephen placed his manuscript into a folder and headed downstairs. He felt a celebration was in order now he had finished his first story. He had read somewhere Stephen King always celebrated the completion of a novel with a bottle of champagne. He looked in the cupboards, no champagne. A good coffee, he decided. He put fresh coffee beans in the grinder and turned it on. He looked through the tins in the cupboard and found an empire biscuit. He ate a small crumb to test it. It was still fresh. He sat there celebrating his achievement with his coffee and biscuit. Today was a great day he said. Outside he heard a noise. It sounded like a car was coming up the driveway - he froze. He heard footsteps on the gravel path walking towards the door. Someone was trying a key in the lock. He stood up and slowly reached towards the chain. The door swung open and his mother stood there carrying some shopping. Stephens heart was racing

'Mum'

'Hi honey. Have you had a good day?' she asked. Sorry, I was mad at you this morning for not going to the job interview. I see you tried to clean up all the pieces of the plate I dropped.

'Sorry mum, I've busy all day. I only left my room ten minutes ago. I've been so busy with my writing.' His mother sat down.

'You look like the cat that's got the cream' she said. Stephen nodded. He picked up his manuscript and slid it across the table.

'I've had the best day ever,' he said.

His mum picked up his manuscript and flicked through it. She saw the two words, 'THE END' typed neatly at the bottom of the last page. She had never seen him do this before.

'Have you actually finished a story?'

Stephen nodded. He was very pleased with himself.

'Make me a coffee, Stephen. I'm going to sit and read this right now.'

Stephen made her a coffee. He picked up the empty washing basket.

'What are you doing with that?' she asked.

'I'm going to bring the washing in.'

She wasn't sure whether to be more shocked at him helping her or that he had finished his story. She sat and read his story from beginning to end. It was exciting. For the first time she knew he really could write.

'You killed me off, how could you? she giggled. Brilliant! Can I buy the first copy?' she asked.

'Just like Theo Van Gogh' 'No. You can have a free copy.' 'Mum, I'm going for that job interview tomorrow'

'What! No, you don't need to. You can write.'

'I need to mum. There are no stories happening in this house. I need material, people, places, gossip, in fact everything to do with a life that will make my stories seem alive. I need to stir my imagination.'

THE END

33
...AND A WHISTLE

THERE ARE SOME MOMENTS IN LIFE THAT DON'T QUITE REGISTER, AT least not immediately. You look at these moments; head cocked to one side while trying to work out what's happening to you, and why you have stopped functioning in your normal way. That's what happened to me on Tuesday morning. I wasn't expecting anything unusual. My life was running mostly the way I wanted it to. Everything was good and seemed to be working just tickety-boo. And ye

. . .

T, there it was, as plain as could be, swinging back and forth in front of me, confusing my head.

I stared straight at it. I knew what it was as I'd seen them at least one hundred times. But even though the familiarity

WAS THERE THIS TIME, it was different. Very different. I could see how my life had changed dramatically in less than a few seconds. The clear hose with its yellow cup attached was swinging back and forth in front of my face. The woman to my left who I'd been deep in conversation with suddenly looked different.

Her face, with her perfect white teeth and beautiful lips, had lost its smile. She stopped talking to me mid-sentence. Her mouth stretched wide, screaming. Her beautiful smile of moments earlier had disappeared. I looked at her again, puzzled, trying to get my head around our situation, but still, her face contorted, a look of terror in her eyes. I didn't get a good look at her eyes earlier during polite conversation, but now, I could see them and it wasn't pretty.

Every day we look at others' faces and see people who are happy, indifferent or sad. We see radiant smiles, sparkling eyes and those memorable teasing looks. The human face expresses so many emotions and yet, this woman's face was different from anything I had ever seen. Her eyes had turned dark and fearful, filled with disbelief and questions, ones I didn't have the answers to. This was a first for me too.

The kid to my right was about eight years old. He wanted the window seat, which I was more than happy to give him. My days of needing to view the world from a plane's window were over.

The boy struggled, trying to release his seatbelt. Unfortunately, he was sat away from his family, a scourge of profit-grabbing airlines. Maybe his family couldn't afford to pay for seats together, and why should they?

I held his seatbelt clasp firmly closed, and hand signalled for him to sit where he was. He tried to wriggle out of the seat to stand up, so I slapped him hard to shock him. He sat still.

I reached forward and grabbed the yellow dangling mouthpiece and pulled the strap over my head, nothing happened. I saw a man two rows in front pulling down on the mask sharply. I pulled twice and immediately the oxygen filled my lungs. The plane's engines screamed at a pitch I'd never heard before. We were falling, uncontrolled, towards the ground.

I leaned across and put the mask on my fellow passenger who was losing consciousness. She started to breathe; her eyes were ever thankful. She grabbed my hand squeezing it harder and harder, her nails digging into my skin. I let her.

I looked at the safety card jutting out of the pocket in front of me. With its safety situations displayed properly in well-drawn graphics. What had the crew said about this type of situation? I couldn't remember but knew it was futile as I had been listening to my music during the safety briefing. Like most flights I've flown I generally ignore the air steward and display an attitude of 'I know better' so I rarely listen to the in-flight safety speech. I didn't need to, did I? I knew it off by heart. But here I am, and I can't remember a damn thing through the confusion.

My fellow passenger was drawing blood from the back of my hand. I leaned over and unclasped her tight grip and took her hand, rubbing it gently, her eyes changed again, tears filled the corners.

The scene unfolding before me was very surreal. The temperature drop and the noise were overwhelming. Items flew around the cabin at high speed, magazines, hand luggage, duty-free bargains, and a small child. They all left through the large gaping hole in the left-hand side of the aircraft. The freezing cold air was the killer. I always travel light and had boarded the plane with nothing but a dress shirt and a pair of loose cargo pants. I looked at the safety card again and nowhere did it say to pack a few warm jumpers in case of a fuselage breach. My shoes were missing from under my seat which bothered me as I had a thing about not being complete without my shoes.

The ice-cold wind penetrated the cabin and pierced my skin, making me shiver, uncontrollably. It may have been the fear of my situation, but I've lived my life never having had a fear of death, which remains true, even in this moment. However, considering the circumstances I find myself in, I understand I hadn't thought about the process of how I would die. I was now in a very uncomfortable situation.

I picked my row wisely on this trip. Well, I didn't actually pick it - I made a choice not to pay an additional fee to have a dedicated seat. I usually prefer the middle of the plane, but this time I was in row thirty-four. Not the best choice as it was too close to the toilets, with its overpowering aroma once in flight. Assessing my situation, it would seem a good choice now as the hole in the fuselage wall was probably around rows fourteen to eighteen.

A bald man dropped onto the floor from his seat. He started to crawl towards the back end of the plane. He was holding on tightly to the bottom of each seat as he shimmied forward. I admired him for still trying to achieve something in his life, especially with the situation we were in.

I wanted to do something too, more than comforting the woman next to me. However, I sat stuck in my seat like the other passengers. We all assumed the frightened rabbit position, sitting still and staring forward.

The man crawling along the floor was struggling against the G-forces pushing against him. His legs were lifting off the floor as he struggled to hold on. A small suitcase fell out of an overhead cabin and bounced along the floor, hitting him square on the head. The case disappeared out through the hole into the blue sky. I leaned over to see if it hurt him. He was no longer there.

The kid next to me was unconscious. He was probably mad at me for slapping him and pushing him back into his seat. I realised he didn't have his mask on and was being starved of oxygen. The safety card said, fix your own mask first and then your child's. But he isn't my child. The airlines should think about situations like this when they separate children from their parents. My dilemma now was real. Do I put his oxygen mask on him, and bring him back to consciousness, or is he best left unaware of our impending doom?

A drinks trolley flew past from the rear galley jamming itself halfway down the aisle sideways. A hand reached over, grabbing a bunch of gin miniatures from the basket. I saw a mask being pulled off; a man drank one after the other while throwing the empty bottles towards the hole. Lucky guy.

Where was the captain when you needed information? No announcement so far. How frustrating when there is a lack of clear information? Maybe he said something; I'm not sure we would hear an announcement above the noise of the screaming engines. If this had been a British Airways flight, I'm sure we would have had some information.

The engine on the right-hand side was billowing out a stream of black smoke. How is it possible we have an engine on the right burning and yet the hole in the fuselage was on the left? I struggled to work it out. Hopefully, the black box was doing its job properly. I had a suspicion we were going to be part of late evening entertainment on some Air Crash Investigation programme. Maybe not. I was still alive and hopefully the pilot and the rest of the cockpit crew were working on a solution up front.

The woman beside me had calmed down slightly. She closed her eyes and was crossing herself, her mouth repeating the same words over and over. She at least knew who she was calling, while I felt slightly awkward. I had given up my religion when I was twenty-three. I wasn't sure now after thirty-odd years of being an atheist if it would be correct for me to change my mind again because of one situation. So for now, I kept with my non-belief and live in the moment beliefs.

A great silence happened upon us. The engines had all cut out, and it was eerily silent apart from a swishing noise from the wind. It felt far better compared to the screaming engines. The noise from them had made it hard to focus.

We were free falling, perhaps even gliding. I wished the pilot would let us know if they were in control. Prayers and wishes broke the silence and lots of crying. Parents heads popped above the headrests, shouting out children's names. There were few replies. There were many, 'Dear Father, forgive me,' calls and 'I don't want to die' making our situation a somewhat sombre occasion.

The kid next to me was still unconscious, and I left him as he was. I wondered if it had been his father who had tried to crawl up the aisle to be with his son. I'm sure in his situation I would have tried it.

The temperature changed, and it became slightly warmer. It was no longer minus 55 degrees and was probably nearer minus 10. In any other circumstance, this wouldn't be a good result but believe me; this temperture was far better.

I'm guessing we must have reached the 10,000 feet level as the pressure was no longer sucking things out the gaping hole. The jagged, twisted hole still framed the corn blue sky, ironically in an artistic way that good a photographer would see.

As we descended, it was difficult to get a decent measure of our height with only ocean below us. As we spun no land was in sight, only water.

I wondered what caused the large hole in the fuselage, and was surprised at how thin the outer skin of our plane was. Had I known they were this thin, I may never have travelled on them.

We were still plummeting towards the sea, my only remaining comfort being I could swim. I felt sorry for any passenger who had never learnt this useful skill. Could we survive hitting the water? Would the Captain be able to glide the plane gently onto the water and if so, would the plane float? Had the crew sent a May-Day signal or were they too busy up front? I was still hoping for an update from the flight deck.

I looked at the safety card again:

Life-jacket. Cross the tires behind your back then bring to front and tie in a bow. OK.

The light. The light should come on automatically if the jacket goes into the water. Hmm, not much use in bright sunshine.

The Whistle. The whistle will allow you to attract the attention of passing ships or other rescue vessels. That's positive. I wondered how loud a sound the whistle would make. Would the crew of a large merchant ship hear my noise above the sound of their engines?

Top-up tube. This tube will keep the life jacket buoyant for many hours. Oh, no! I've found my fear. With my weight being close to eighteen stone the life-jacket I observed the stewardess wearing during the briefing looked too flimsy. While listening to my iPhone, I caught sight of her in the bright yellow jacket. I thought at the time it wasn't big enough to keep her afloat, and she looked only nine stone.

I needed to remember all these instructions. I wondered if I could stand at the edge of the hole and jump out a couple of seconds before we hit the water. Could I jump up the way to break my fall a bit? I wasn't sure.

The answer to the pilot gliding the plane to the surface of the water came forward itself. The aircraft banked heavily to one side and then started to spin. It was slow at first and then turned into my worst nightmare. It brought back childhood memories of bad times stuck on fairground waltzers.

I heard a click behind me, and the toilet door opened. A stewardess stood there surveying the scene. She went to the back of the plane, and I listened as she called out to the captain on the intercom. There was no reply. She made her way down the aisle pushing the drinks trolley aside. She walked remarkably well considering we were spinning. She passed the hole without getting sucked out. A twenty-something-year-old girl sat nearest the hole, got out of her seat. She climbed over two rows of seats and headed back towards us and locked herself in the loo.

My fellow passenger leant over and hugged me tightly. She removed her mask and told me to tell her things would be OK, I nodded. My first lie to her and I didn't even know her. She kissed me on the cheek. I could feel the wetness of her face against mine as we sat cheek to cheek. Across the aisle, a man was writing his last goodbye or perhaps an account of the whole horrid scene onto his laptop. No doubt he hoped his message to friends and family would survive the crash.

The chief stewardess was joined by another crew member. The both banged frantically on the cockpit door. Regarding their training for staying calm in front of the passengers, let's just say it wasn't convincing. The second stewardess picked up the phone and tried talking to the cockpit once more, but again, no answer.

She smacked the phone against the wall, and the system came to life with a bit of a crackle.

'We seem to have a problem,' she said, crying into the phone. Her years of training had kicked in with the right words, but losing her emotions told a different story.

A man screamed at the stewardesses blaming them for what had happened. It's sad in a moment like this, some shallow-minded idiot has to apportion blame. When will people realise sometimes life is just the way it is? The boy beside me didn't wake up. We spun for another fifteen seconds….

34

INDEPENDENCE

It doesn't matter what they do or say
It doesn't matter how hard they try
The taste of freedom runs wild amongst us
Independence! Our people cry

CONTACT ME

Hi Everyone,

I hope you enjoyed this collection and would like to read more. "More," you cry, yes unfortunately I have lots more much to your dismay. He he!

Sign up for my no-spam newsletter on my website where I give insights into what I'm working on, as well as some exclusive content which I send first to my subscribers.

You can also follow me on the following Social Media platforms:

Facebook.com/GrahameAnderson

Website - grahameanderson.com

Instagram - @grahameanderson

Printed in Great Britain
by Amazon

43386438R00076